JAMES CLYDE AND THE DIAMONDS OF ORCHESTRA

Colm McElwain

Matador
9 Priory Busines Park
Wistow Road
Kibworth Beauchamp
Leicester LE8 0RX, UK
Tel: 0116 279 2299
Email: books@troubador.co.uk
Web: www.troubador.co.uk/matador

ISBN 978 1 78088 069 3

British Library Cataloguing in Publication Data.
A catalogue record for this book is available from the British Library.

Typeset in 11pt Aldine by Troubador Publishing Ltd, Leicester, UK
Printed and bound in the UK by TJ International, Padstow, Cornwall

Matador is an imprint of Troubador Publishing Ltd

With the Support of Monaghan Arts Council

Cover illustration by Jon Donohoe

www.jamesclydebook.com

Prologue

Marcus Baker ran as fast as he could through the Darken forest, constantly glancing over his shoulder as he went. The trees around him towered into the sky and their branches arched and met in the middle, allowing only sporadic shafts of silvery moonlight through.

At 20 years old, Marcus didn't require much light. He was lean and fast, with a good knowledge of the terrain over which he ran. He leapt over a fallen tree, feeling his tattered boots sinking into the soil.

As he surveyed the misty forest, he could understand why some would never enter it. Sometimes referred to as "The Forest of the Dead", the woods had always been synonymous with evil spirits and magical diamonds. Moreover, the atmosphere was still and silent, like a graveyard in the middle of the night.

And yet to Marcus, this was home. He knew the forest better than anyone and tonight, strangers were here with him. It was impossible to say who they were, but he was definitely being followed.

Finally, out of breath, he stopped and adjusted the strap of the brown satchel that hung around his neck. Then, dropping to his knees, he hid behind the nearest tree, listening.

Soon there came sounds of twigs snapping and he could see light flickering in the distance. Remaining perfectly still, he tried to make out the figure approaching.

At first, all he could see was the light of the candle growing larger, but then an elderly man stepped into view.

The man was dressed strangely, wearing a blue robe that stretched out behind him like a wedding dress. His face was lined and covered with a white beard so long that it almost touched the hem of his robe.

Several feet away, numerous more figures emerged from the trees.

An angry voice spoke. 'Where did he go?'

'You lost him?'

'We all lost him.'

The old man blew out the candle. 'He can't have gotten far. Find him. Kill him!'

Marcus could feel his heart pounding. *Who are these people? Why do they want me dead?* He had no wealth, no connections to the king. He was simply a farmer's son.

As quietly as possible, he sprinted in the direction of his kingdom. He would find safety there.

For several minutes he ran, stopping only occasionally to make sure he hadn't been followed. Each time, the forest was still and quiet. This was promising, but he had taken no chances.

During his last stop, he had hooked the strap of his bag on to a protruding branch and run in the opposite direction. A decoy. It would send his assailants in the other direction – or at the very least give him some extra time.

Happy with his progress, he now maintained his frantic pace, side stepping trees as he hurried. Moments later he paused, breathless, hoping he had lost his pursuers.

The lights of the kingdom were now in sight. Two more minutes should see him home. He was about to run when he heard a dull thud. Standing still, he looked left and right, his eyes full of fear.

Through the blanket of mist, he could see very little. Nothing seemed out of place – the leaves of the trees stirred in the breeze, but there was nothing peculiar there. Then, out of the corner of his eye, he saw his shoulder bag lying on the ground.

It was hardly recognisable: the fabric was in tatters and the strap was cut in half. Knees trembling, he walked slowly forward. *I have to get out of here! They're getting closer.*

He turned his body to run, but before he could take another step, he felt a quick stab of pain. Looking down, he saw a sword inside his stomach and a small stain of black blood forming on his shirt.

For a moment, shock numbed the pain.

Then he looked up at his attacker.

The eyes peering back at him were crimson red, almost like a demon's. He gave a guttural groan and pain laced with panic arrived in equal measure.

In desperation, he groped at the blade impaled in his stomach, trying to remove it, but the claws holding the hilt shoved the steel further inside, denying him any chance of survival.

The wound was now grave. He knew it, and the towering creature staring back at him knew it too. He turned away, his eyes focusing on the thatched cottages of the kingdom.

He found his own house – the Baker cottage, taller than the rest, with a long chimney billowing smoke into the air.

Happy memories came flooding back: days spent playing with his brother on the farm, gathering vegetables for the dinner and the time his father taught him how to plough the land.

His last thought before he took his final breath, however, was of his deceased mother, welcoming him home with open arms.

She stood at the threshold of their house and looked exactly like he remembered her: there was no sign of the terrible illness that had claimed her life many years before. She was smiling at him and beckoning him towards her.

Marcus went to her and she embraced him warmly. They held each other for a moment and then she offered her hand.

Marcus didn't even have to think about it; he smiled at his mother, took her hand and walked beside her as she led him away.

Two miles further back, the elderly man stood patiently, waiting for developments.

From amongst the trees, a hulking man appeared and knelt reverentially before the blue-robed man. 'Most of the Volens have started digging, Your Lordship, but there is nothing to report as yet.'

The man nodded, stroking his beard. 'Patience. We'll locate it eventually.'

The Volen shook his head. 'You're sure they exist? They're only legend, after all. There's no evidence to support the theory of diamonds in this forest.'

'They exist.' The old man nodded to the ground. 'Somewhere beneath us lies one diamond.'

'One! Not three?'

'Two are in Zara.'

The Volen's eyes narrowed. 'How do you know this?'

'Trust me, my good man,' the old man replied.

The Volen looked at the distant lights of the kingdom. 'Might I make a suggestion?'

'Please do.'

The Volen smiled, his black tongue flickering like some terrible serpent. 'We should attack the castle immediately,' he said robustly. 'King Epson would be vulnerable tonight.'

The old man shrugged. 'Perhaps you're right,' he said. 'Bring me the king's head and I'll see you rewarded.'

The Volen gave an assured nod and strode away.

Looking down, the old man's gaze fell on the leafy ground, where a puddle remained from a heavy shower of rain earlier in the day. With a smile, he knelt, seeming to take great pleasure in his own reflection. A moment later, he rose and called out, 'Stop, we won't have to attack!'

The Volen turned, surprised. 'I strongly suggest we make a

move during the night hours. As I've already said, King Epson won't be expecting it.'

The old man glanced down at the puddle once more, as if to double check something. Slowly, his smile developed into a grin. He was sure. 'You don't understand,' he said. 'We won't have to breach the castle at all.'

The Volen shook his head. 'I don't understand.'

Raising his white eyebrows, the man looked at the Volen and said, 'King Epson of Darken is *already* dead.'

PART 1

- CHAPTER ONE -

James Clyde

As quickly as he could, James Clyde unzipped his sports jacket and stuffed three pairs of scarves, hats and gloves inside. He looked left and right, hoping he hadn't been spotted.

Aside from one curious look from a middle-aged woman, he seemed to have gotten away with it. Staying calm, he disappeared behind a display of designer suits and made his way towards the exit doors.

Not surprisingly, a uniformed security guard was standing by the doors, but James smiled to himself when he saw the young man peering in the opposite direction. He desperately wanted to run, but such a move would look suspicious. Finally, he came to the exit doors and walked quickly through.

At once, his walk developed into a furious sprint. The alarm system had been activated, and the security guard was giving chase.

'First floor,' shouted the guard into a walkie-talkie. 'I repeat – suspected shoplifter on first floor, moving towards the main exit.'

The walkie-talkie crackled with static.

'What does he look like?' a voice barked back finally.

'Suspect's about 10 years old, wearing a blue sports jacket, black jogging trousers and white trainers.'

'Exit already blocked. Lead him towards it.'

'Understood.' The guard attached the walkie-talkie to his belt and hurried along the walkway.

James, alarmed by what he had just overheard, took a sharp left to a staircase. Up he went, swinging his arms back and forth, generating speed as he moved in between the bodies around him.

Reaching the top, he peered around. It was a late evening in December and the shopping centre was extremely busy. He was just about to start running again when he heard the sound of heavy footsteps. Turning, he saw the security guard standing at the foot of the stairs, looking angrily up at him.

'There's no way out, son. Give it up!'

James shrugged. 'Sorry. You'll just have to try and keep up. Or you could stop chasing me!' With that, he turned and began to run, the numerous department stores passing swiftly by.

Rounding the next corner, he shuffled past people of all shapes and sizes, pushing aside anyone who got in his way. Then, using his shoulder, he crashed though a side door and found himself in a wide area full of noisy shoppers. He stopped, panting, looking in all directions.

Up ahead, in the centre of the walkway, a magician had his audience captivated with his wide-ranging tricks. A little further on, a boy, perhaps the same age as himself, was getting his portrait drawn by an artist.

On his right was a rather fancy looking restaurant, where a group of elderly men sat sipping coffee and talking loudly to one another. Then his attention was caught by a long line of people, mostly teenage girls, queuing outside a small wooden hut covered with purple curtains.

James heaved a sigh. He briefly considered staying where he was – perhaps he could simply blend into the crowd – but something told him the sooner he left, the better.

It was then that his eye was drawn to an exit sign just past the magic show. This was his chance. Quickly, he made his move, but as he did so, the exit door swung open and a large man wearing a navy-blue uniform came walking through.

While the last security guard was small and slightly overweight, this latest one was strong and athletic.

Diving for cover behind a wall, James could feel the sweat forming on his brow. He had no desire to stay where he was and be caught, but he couldn't go back downstairs.

He had to hide. Somewhere. Anywhere!

He looked again at the restaurant. Could there be a back door? His mind was racing. Would the security guard check in there? Suddenly, he noticed that the people who had been queuing outside the curtained hut were no longer there. *Perfect!*

Aware that the security guard was getting closer, he dashed across the walkway towards the hut. Keeping low, he rushed inside, pulling the curtains behind him. It took a moment for him to find his bearings as the lighting in the room was very dim.

Ahead was a small wooden table, covered with a satin cloth. On either side were two high-backed chairs. A guttering candle and a small crystal bowl were positioned in the middle of the table.

Turning, James parted the curtains through which he had entered. Outside, the magic show was still continuing and there was no sign of any security guards patrolling the walkways. It did seem highly unlikely that the guard would still be in the same area, but he would take no chances. He would wait here for another few minutes, then leave.

With a great sense of relief, he moved further into the room. The smell of coffee in the air was almost overpowering and the wooden floor on which he walked creaked with every step he took.

On his right was a filing cabinet with a series of drawers, and at the other end of the room there was a kitchen area with pots and pans stacked inside a sink.

Hanging on the walls were six framed newspaper cuttings. Curious, he walked around the room, his eyes studying the titles:

THE GREAT BELINDA, THE CELEBRATED FORTUNE TELLER, DOES IT AGAIN!

BELINDA, FORTUNE TELLER EXTRAORDINAIRE, HELPS FIND MISSING CHILD ALIVE AND WELL!

THE GREAT BELINDA: PSYCHIC OR PSYCHOTIC?

'I'm sorry, my dear,' came a voice from the shadows, 'I'm closed for the day.'

James jumped. 'Sorry.' He turned to leave, but before he could make it to the curtains, the woman spoke.

'Just a moment. What is your name?'

James turned to face the woman. 'I'm James. Are you Belinda?'

The woman smiled. 'Most of the time.'

James could now see the woman standing by the table, rooting inside her handbag. She was young, perhaps in her late 20s, with brown hair tied back in a bun.

'Now then, why would a boy your age want to visit a fortune teller?' asked Belinda.

James shook his head. 'I was just looking around.'

Belinda smiled. 'You weren't thinking of stealing something?'

'No!' said James, trying to sound convincing.

Belinda pulled out a chair beside the table. 'Now, my dear, take a seat.'

'Why?'

Belinda nodded to a newspaper clipping on the wall, the one with the headline:

THE GREAT BELINDA, THE CELEBRATED FORTUNE TELLER, DOES IT AGAIN!

James turned to leave again. 'Er, no thanks.' He patted his pockets. 'I've no money.'

'On the house,' replied Belinda.

James shrugged, thinking hard.

Belinda said, 'It won't take long, I assure you.'

James looked back at the curtain, then at the table. Perhaps it wasn't such a bad idea; staying in here for a few more minutes would guarantee his safety. 'Okay then.'

'Good,' said Belinda with a broad smile. 'Won't this be fun?'

James smiled as he sat down. The bowl before him on the table had a small amount of water inside and strangely there was a flick knife beside it.

There was a long silence before Belinda sat down.

James looked at her and said, 'You're very young to be a fortune teller.'

Belinda's smile vanished, and James could tell he had said something to annoy her.

Belinda stared at him. 'And you're very young to be a shoplifter.'

James, swinging back on his chair, nearly fell off. 'What?' He quickly tried to get up, but Belinda grabbed his wrist, lifted the flick knife and brought it towards his index finger.

'What are you doing?' cried James, shaking his hand, trying to break free.

'Don't struggle,' said Belinda calmly. 'It will only make it worse.'

'Make *what* worse?'

'This might hurt a little.' And then she flicked the knife.

CHAPTER TWO

A Special Boy

James grimaced. 'Ouch! You cut me!'

Belinda frowned at him. 'It's barely a scratch.'

'You could've warned me,' James told her.

'And what purpose would that have served?'

'Why did you do that?' James took a handkerchief out of his pocket and wrapped it around his finger.

'Don't do that!' cried Belinda.

'Why not?'

'I need your blood.'

'Excuse me?'

Belinda held the bowl in the air. 'Quick, hold your finger over the water.'

Sucking his finger, James shook his head.

Belinda sighed. 'Look, James, your finger is already cut. Why turn back now?'

Reluctantly, James held out his finger and watched as three droplets of his blood fell into the bowl, mixing with the water.

'Good,' said Belinda. 'Now, was that so hard?'

While Belinda stared into the bowl, James looked back again at the half-dozen newspaper articles hanging on the walls. His eye was caught by one that seemed appropriate now:

THE GREAT BELINDA: PSYCHIC OR PSYCHOTIC?

It's a good question, James thought. She was certainly odd. There was no disputing that, but she was also strangely likeable. He took a closer look at Belinda, who was now moving the bowl from side to side, as though she were a child trying to find an extra cornflake at the very bottom.

'All done,' said Belinda, placing the bowl back down on the table.

James smiled. 'Really? Already?' He eased back into his chair, expecting to hear some vague garbage about being into sports, computer games and action movies.

Belinda cleared her throat and made eye contact with him. 'Your second name is Clyde.'

James's eyes widened with interest. 'How did you know that?'

'Please let me finish.'

'Sorry.'

'You're an orphan, but have recently been adopted by a woman called Anne Brown. However, you spend every Christmas with your grandfather Wilmore, who lives in a big old house in the country. You've an adopted brother and sister called Ben and Mary, both of whom you met at the children's home.' She looked at James. 'Ring any bells?'

James was sitting up now. 'You're right. But how do you – ?'

Belinda held a hand in the air. 'James, you and your family are in terrible danger. I sense there is a man trying to find you. He's trying to hurt you!'

James nodded, cringing. 'The security guard,' he told her. 'I might've borrowed a couple of items from the clothes shop downstairs, but you have to understand that I was desperate. You see, it's the middle of winter and we sleep in a room that's freezing cold.'

'It's not the guard,' Belinda told him.

James leaned closer. 'Who then?'

'Another man,' said Belinda softly. 'This man has been trying to find you for some time. He feels you're a threat.'

'I'm a threat,' said James. 'Why? How?'

Belinda went across the room and carried back with her a jug of water. Then she began to pour, filling the bowl to the brim. 'Let's find out, shall we?' She dipped her finger into the water and watched as a small ripple went across the surface. The droplets of blood had now vanished and the water seemed clear. 'Where were you born, James?' she asked after a long moment.

James narrowed his eyes. 'In a hospital,' he replied.

Belinda gave him a puzzled look. 'What hospital?'

James shrugged.

Belinda raised one eyebrow. 'You don't know, do you?'

James's face reddened.

'Don't you think it's strange that nobody has ever mentioned the place of your birth?' added Belinda.

James shook his head. 'Why would that be strange? A hospital isn't exactly –'

'You weren't born in a hospital,' Belinda told him. 'Neither were you born on Earth.'

'Huh?' James was lost. 'Are you saying that I'm an alien from outer space?'

A wide smile formed on Belinda's face. 'Not quite.'

'Where was I born then?' asked James, interested now.

'Are you sure you want to know?' replied Belinda darkly.

James was smiling. A different newspaper clipping had just caught his eye:

LOCAL PSYCHIC PREDICTED AIRCRAFT DISASTER: NO SURVIVORS!

'Well, do you?'

James lifted his finger. 'It's already cut, so why turn back now?'

Belinda smiled at him. 'Very well.' Carefully, she trickled two drops of water into the bowl and gazed inside. A moment later, she was grinning to herself. 'Why, James Clyde, you are a special boy!'

CHAPTER THREE

The Escape

Having finished his "psychic" reading, James could feel the cold water rolling down his face and dripping underneath the collar of his jacket. He splashed his face again, turned off the tap and stared at his reflection in the large mirror.

He had blue eyes and short brown hair, spiked by a dab of gel which he applied religiously every morning. He was a normal height and weight for a boy of 11 years and six months and he certainly didn't feel any different.

Nor did he ever want to be. He was quite happy to be like everybody else, thank you very much.

And yet, in his mind he still thought about everything that Belinda had said to him. He was special; destined for greatness, destined to be a great leader. She seemed to know everything. Could she be wrong once?

Suddenly, the door of the toilets swung open. 'You're going to jail, you little thief!'

James turned, smiling. 'Ben, if I go down, you're coming with me.'

Ben Forester was 10 years old, two inches smaller in height than James, but about the same weight. His black hair, once curly and long, was now cut short, and his features were practically hidden behind a pair of oversized glasses. 'C'mon, let's get out of here.'

'What took you so long?' asked James, pacing towards the door. 'I almost got caught.'

'Brown,' replied Ben with a sigh.

James groaned. 'What has she done now?'

Ben shook his head. 'Well, after doing the dishes I had to study for three hours. Study! Me! I think she's trying to lay down some ground rules. She wouldn't let me leave until I had mastered algebra.'

'And did you?' said James.

'Nah, I got Mary to do them for me.'

'Good thinking.'

Ben nodded. 'Yeah, to be fair, she came up trumps yet again.'

Together, they opened the door and looked out at the different shops.

'No sign of him,' said James, looking over at Ben.

Ben shook his head, knocking his glasses on to the bridge of his nose. 'Er, who are we supposed to be looking for?'

'A security guard almost caught me,' said James with a smile. 'Well, two actually.'

Ben took off his glasses and started to squint, as he often did in tense situations. 'Perfect.'

'Relax,' said James. 'He's long gone.'

Ben was suddenly grinning, looking at James. 'I have something to ask you.'

'It's not about algebra, is it?'

'Nope.'

'Good. What then?'

'I was just wondering – if I'm the good-looking one, and Mary's the smart one, what does that make you?'

'Hey, you two!' shouted an angry voice. 'Hold it right there.'

With a jump, James spun around. Through the crowd, he saw the heavier of the two security guards standing with his arms by his side, an angry look upon his face.

James winked at Ben. 'I'm the fast one.' Then he broke into a sprint, passing people as he made his way towards an exit.

Ben started to run as fast as he could. 'Wait for me!' he cried, trying to keep up.

And with that, without ever stopping or looking back, they both barged through the exit doors, down the staircase and out into the cold showery night.

- CHAPTER FOUR -

Mary Forester

James put the clothes that were under his jacket down beside the rest of the laundry, then looked at Ben. 'She'll never know.'

'Never know what, exactly?' said a sharp voice. Suddenly, the door of the kitchen swung open and Anne Brown came walking through like a cowboy entering a saloon.

She was a tall, slim woman of about 50, with short grey hair and eyes as black as a storm cloud. 'An explanation, please,' she said, tapping her wrist watch. 'It's well after nine.'

'Er, we went into town,' said Ben. 'Very nice. Late shopping tonight. Plenty of people about, too.'

'Without permission?' Brown shook her head. 'I can't accept that. Do you both understand me?'

'Sure,' said Ben under his breath.

'I beg your pardon?'

'Yes, Miss Brown,' Ben corrected.

'That's better,' said Brown. 'From this moment onwards, you're to be in this house at all times until I state otherwise. Do I make myself clear?'

James nodded, then Ben.

'Now, Mary has just gone to bed. I suggest you both do likewise.'

'Bed?' James raised his eyebrows. 'But it's only half past nine.'

'And?'

'Well, that's a little early for us,' Ben told her. 'We generally wouldn't go until well after 11. We usually watch telly around this time.'

'Not anymore,' replied Brown in a strong tone of voice. 'Upstairs!'

Doing as they were told, James and Ben left the kitchen and made their way up the steep staircase in the middle of the hallway.

Reaching the top, they entered their room and looked around. Things had noticeably improved. Fresh flowers had replaced dead ones, a large radiator had been added and the wooden floor had been swept.

As expected, Mary Forester was lying asleep in one of the beds.

Ben looked at James and whispered, 'It could be worse, couldn't it?'

'I suppose,' James whispered back. 'It's still cold though, isn't it?'

'Freezing,' said Ben, walking over to his bed at the far side of the room, the one nearest the window.

James went over to Mary's bed, sat down and waved a hand in front of her eyes, checking for a reaction. 'You don't fool me, you know?' he said after a moment.

Mary, a small, blonde-haired girl with freckles, opened her eyes with a giggle. 'How did you know?'

James laughed. 'You smiled.'

'No, I didn't.'

James nodded. 'Yeah, you did.'

Sitting up, Mary laid her head on James's shoulder. 'Do you like it here, James?'

James shook his head. 'She's not a very nice woman, is she?'

'She's just horrible,' replied Mary. 'She made me wash the dishes after supper.'

Ben was laughing. 'She doesn't like doing them, does she?'

James managed a smile. 'Listen, let's give her a chance.'

Ben lay down on his bed, removed his glasses and placed them on his bedside locker. 'Right then, we'll give her a chance. Just the one, mind you.'

'Why can't we stay with Wilmore, anyway?' asked Mary.

'I don't know,' James told her. Taking off his jacket, he placed it over Mary. 'Maybe we will one day.'

Mary's eyes lit up. 'Do you really think so?'

Ben looked skeptical. 'Nope.'

'Why not?' said Mary, looking angrily over at Ben.

'Listen, blondie, he doesn't want us,' said Ben.

Mary looked devastated. 'That's not true!'

'What else could it be?' asked Ben in an aggressive tone of voice.

'Any number of reasons,' said Mary.

'Like what?' Ben shook his head. 'Listen, Mary, if Wilmore really wanted us to stay with him, then we would be.'

'We're staying with him next week, aren't we?' Mary pointed out.

Ben ruffled his pillow. 'For two weeks,' he said. 'That's just terrific.'

Mary looked at James and said, 'Wilmore would love to have us, wouldn't he?'

James walked over to his bed, lay down and looked up at the ceiling. 'Yes, of course he would,' he said finally.

Feeling better, Mary smiled and placed her head back on to the pillow.

James turned on to his side, feeling annoyed with himself. But what else could he have said? He made himself a promise there and then – he would never lie to Mary Forester again.

- CHAPTER FIVE -

The Mystery

That night, James was woken by the sound of classical music. Cursing under his breath, he waited for a few minutes, hoping the music would stop. When it didn't, he sat up and looked at his surroundings. The red digits on his bedside alarm clock read: 3.06 A.M. What was going on?

He fumbled for his slippers beside the bed and put them on. Fighting the exhaustion, he walked across the room and, opening the door quietly, went out into the gloomy corridor.

He stood there for a moment, listening. He could hear muffled voices, and there was a definite reduction in the music's noise level. *Bit late,* he thought.

Fully awake now, he descended the stairs. When he came to the bottom, he noticed that the living room door hadn't closed fully. A shaft of gold light broke through the gap and he went quickly towards it.

Ever so quietly, he got down on his hands and knees, anxious to hear every word that was being said.

The only light in the room was coming from the fireplace and Anne Brown was striding up and down the carpet, a glass of wine in her hand. 'Symphony *No 40 in G minor,*' she said to a person James could not yet see.

'More wine, Veronica?' said Brown.

'Not for me, thanks.'

Brown lifted the bottle of wine from the coffee table and took a swig. 'A remarkable vintage, don't you think?'

James glimpsed the woman named Veronica. Pushing his head closer, he looked through the crack where the door hadn't shut fully and saw a plump woman warming herself beside the fireplace.

'So, about these children,' said Veronica.

Holding his breath, James moved a fraction closer to the door.

Brown drew a prolonged sigh. 'What a disaster that has been,' she replied. 'I wanted three boys, but I got landed with a young girl. Troubled children, all three of them.'

'Really?'

Brown shrugged. 'Well, perhaps I'm being unfair. They haven't had the best of starts in life. The youngest two – Ben and Mary – are brother and sister, but the eldest, James, has no family at all.'

'How tragic.'

Brown crossed the room and decanted another bottle of wine before topping up her glass. 'Yes, it's very sad. A young lady at the children's home told me the entire story. Ben and Mary were found soaking wet on the stone slabs outside the home.'

'Just lying there?'

Brown nodded her head sadly. 'Abandoned by their parents, just lying there in the rain, with only their names pinned to their clothes.'

There was a silence in the room, only broken by the crackling of the logs in the grate.

'And what of the other one?' said the woman named Veronica. 'James, is it?'

'James, yes,' replied Brown. 'Well, his arrival at the children's home was every bit as mysterious. It was a rainy night in June when his grandfather arrived at the doors –'

'I thought you said he had no family.'

'Well, he doesn't really. You see, his grandfather, Wilmore Clyde, is a strange man. Unstable. Almost 12 years ago, he arrived at the children's home holding a baby in his arms – his grandson, James.'

'What's odd about that?'

Brown put down the glass. 'He was covered in blood, Veronica.'

'Blood?'

'That's right,' said Brown with a nod. 'Man and child were soaked in blood. Wilmore Clyde was moments from death that night.'

'And what about James?'

'Unharmed. The blood was entirely Wilmore's.'

'What the hell happened to him?'

Brown shook her head. 'To this day, nobody knows – nobody apart from Wilmore Clyde, that is. Strange, wouldn't you say?'

'Strange! It's an outrage!'

Brown was nodding. 'Isn't it just? I've yet to meet the man, but I'm told he's a virtual recluse. He lives in a huge house in the countryside somewhere.'

'With any luck, that's where he'll stay.'

'I'm afraid not,' said Brown. 'He's collecting the children tomorrow. They're spending Christmas with him.'

'And you allowed this?'

'I had no say in the matter,' said Brown with a shake of her head. 'They've always stayed with him at Christmas.'

The music's volume increased again and James took two tentative steps back from the door. He was trembling. The conversation he had just overheard had thrown his world into chaos.

Running up the stairs two steps at a time, he returned to his bed, but he never slept. His overactive mind saw to that. He just lay in his bed, staring at the ceiling, imagining the supposed scene of his arrival at the home.

After weighing everything up, he was having trouble believing a drunken stranger over his grandfather. There had to be some other explanation.

Yes, Anne Brown was simply misinformed. There were

hundreds of children at the home. Perhaps another child had arrived in such strange circumstances, but not him.

Not him!

He closed his eyes and sleep eventually took its welcome hold. But every so often throughout the night, he would wake for a moment, and when he did one question still nagged above any other – what if it *was* true?

CHAPTER SIX

Looking for James

The next morning brought unexpected snow – the heaviest fall seen in the area for over 25 years. Word came through, however, that school would be going ahead as planned.

'Isn't that good news?' said Brown as she hurried around the kitchen, making sure that every switch and tap was turned off.

'I suppose,' said Ben, eating his cereal. 'What was all that music last night?'

Brown smiled and topped up Ben's juice. 'That was Wolfgang Amadeus Mozart, the brilliant composer, who was born in Salzburg in 1756.'

Ben lowered his spoon. 'What was he doing in the living room at three in the morning, then? Did you hear it, Jimbo?'

James shrugged. 'Dunno.'

'I didn't hear a thing,' said Mary happily, buttering her toast.

Ben wiped the lenses of his glasses with a napkin. 'Well, good for you,' he said. 'That's just made my day!'

'That's quite enough,' said Brown, glancing at her wrist watch. 'Now, everyone please get a move on. I'll be out in the car. Don't forget your schoolbags.'

Robbing the toast out of Mary's hand, Ben lifted his schoolbag and ran out into the hallway. 'C'mon, Mary, try and keep up.'

'Ben, did you get your maths homework done?' Mary called out.

Brown nodded. 'He certainly did. I checked it myself. There wasn't a single sum wrong.'

Ben smiled up at Brown. 'Algebra's easy enough once you've got the hang of it.'

'Practice makes perfect, young Benjamin,' said Brown, waving him out the front door.

Arm in arm, James and Mary left the kitchen. Then, after closing and locking the front door, they jumped into Brown's black car. 10 minutes later, they arrived at school.

★

It was the last day of school before the Christmas holidays. The avenue at the bottom of the school was crowded with children, all of whom appeared eager to get into class as they hurried from their buses, striking one another with the occasional snowball.

James, Ben and Mary ascended the steep lane and made their way into class, taking their seats as usual beside a boy called Simon Rainbow and a girl named Jane Locke.

Simon was a plump, red-faced child who children cruelly likened to the Disney cartoon character 'Porky Pig'.

At exactly 12.30 P.M, Mr Brody, the school principal, rang the lunch bell. The sound of children's shoes stamping on the tiled floor outside rebounded loudly into Mrs Walsh's classroom.

'And we're out of here!' cried Simon suddenly, throwing his maths book to the floor.

'How dare you, Simon,' barked Mrs Walsh. 'I never said class was over.'

'Eh?'

Putting on a pair of glasses, Mrs Walsh rose from her chair. 'Class is not over until I say so!'

Simon jumped. 'But Miss, that's the bell.'

'That bell is to let *me* know it's break time, not you,' said Mrs Walsh, her tone very firm.

'Yes, Miss,' replied Simon, stooping to lift his book.

Mrs Walsh said very authoritatively, 'I will ask you your 12 times tables when class resumes after break. For your own sake, I hope you've learned them.'

James looked at Simon, who sneakily mouthed the words, 'I forgot.'

'*Now* you may go out for your lunch,' said Mrs Walsh, smiling around at the rest of the class.

All the children in the class moved towards the door apart from Simon, who lifted his lunchbox and looked at James nervously.

'James Clyde,' said Mrs Walsh unexpectedly, 'could I see you for a minute, please?'

'I'll be out in a minute, Simon,' said James, who then walked in the direction of the teacher's desk while Simon pouted outside, cursing the lack of sweets available to him in his packed lunchbox.

Assuming he was in some sort of trouble, James approached Mrs Walsh's desk with trepidation. Before he arrived, however, Mrs Walsh jumped from her seat, lifted a piece of chalk and wrote the words 12 TIMES TABLES in block capitals at the very top of the blackboard.

'You wanted to see me, Miss?' said James in a low voice.

Mrs Walsh walked back to her seat, sat down, lowered her glasses on to the bridge of her nose and arched her eyebrows. 'Yes, James, I just wanted to let you know that there was a man here looking for you yesterday.'

James drew a long breath. 'Oh, was it my grandfather?'

'No, it wasn't your grandfather.' Mrs Walsh shook her head. 'In fact, I've never seen this man before in my life, but I found him a little strange so I didn't tell him where you lived or anything like that.'

James nodded. 'Okay.'

Mrs Walsh removed her glasses, looked at James and said, 'This man arrived at school at the end of the day when you had just gone home.'

As she told James about the strange visitor, Mrs Walsh began to see again in her mind's eye the unsettling way in which the man had stared at her.

'Can you tell me where James Clyde lives, then?' he had asked. The question had struck her as strange and she wondered about that at the time. Surely a friend of the family ought to know the address? But when she had pointed this out, the stranger had looked uncomfortable and mumbled something which she did not hear, before leaving shortly afterwards without further explanation.

The whole episode had left her feeling distinctly uneasy and she had made up her mind to ask James about it at the very first opportunity.

'Have you any idea who this man could've been?' she asked him now.

'Not really,' James told her. 'What did he look like?'

Mrs Walsh looked up at the ceiling. 'Let me see, I guess he was in his 60s, smartly dressed, softly spoken.' She rubbed her chin with her chalky fingers. 'I particularly remember his coat.'

'His coat?'

'Yes. He had a long black coat that ran to his ankles. What else? Erm, he had thinning hair and a bushy moustache.'

There was a brief silence, during which time Mrs Walsh rubbed her strained eyes. 'Well, any ideas?'

Mrs Walsh had given him a wonderful description, but James was still no clearer. 'None,' he told her.

Mrs Walsh waved it off. 'I'm sure it was nothing, James,' she said, putting her glasses back on, 'but I just wanted to tell you about him.'

'Well, thanks anyway,' said James. 'May I go?'

'You may,' said Mrs Walsh, and James turned and sprinted outside.

★

'What was that all about, then?' asked Simon, who was in the middle of the courtyard.

James smiled, knowing he couldn't miss an opportunity like this. 'She wanted my advice on how long a student should get suspended for if he threw a maths book on the floor.'

Simon gasped.

'I'm only joking,' said James. 'It was nothing. Somebody was looking for me yesterday, that's all.' When James saw the worried look still lingering on Simon's face, he decided to change the subject. 'So, Simon, any plans for Christmas?'

'My family are going on holidays and I have to go with them,' said Simon, with a frown. 'We're visiting my grandparents along the way.'

James shrugged. 'What's wrong with that?'

Simon rolled his eyes. 'My grandmother always forces me to eat these horrible sweets. I have to pretend to love them, but when she's not looking I always sneak outside and spit them out.'

Laughing, James flung an arm around Simon. 'C'mon, let's find Ben and Mary.'

CHAPTER SEVEN

Wilmore Clyde

Later that day, Mary stood outside Brown's house, waiting for Wilmore to arrive. As expected, there was a great deal of snow covering the ground and, although it had stopped, a chill still languished in the December air. Even so, nothing could stop her waiting.

Suddenly, a car horn honked twice and two shafts of gold light broke through the darkness. Even before she saw the car, she knew who it was. 'Wilmore!' she shouted, running quickly forward and leaving a trail in the snow.

Wilmore Clyde got quickly out of his car, eager to see Mary Forester. He was an exceptionally big man with tightly-cropped grey hair and twinkling green eyes that shrunk in size whenever he laughed.

Dressed in a long brown coat that covered a tweed suit, he looked a good 10 years younger than his 65 years.

'Wilmore,' said Mary, hugging him. 'You're here.'

'Mary, my dear!' cried Wilmore, lifting her high into the air and swinging her around like a little doll.

Despite not liking heights, Mary always felt very safe in Wilmore's arms. Lost for words, she smiled down at him.

'Look how much you've grown,' said Wilmore, grinning.

Mary frowned at him. 'Wilmore, I'm still the smallest in my class.'

'And a good thing you are, too!' said Wilmore. 'We don't want you growing up too quickly now, do we?' He gazed around. 'Where are the boys?'

Mary's face had lit up again. 'They're inside.'

Wilmore winked at her. 'Let's go and get them.' Holding Mary tightly in his arms, he made his way towards the door of the house.

At that moment, James and Ben came running out of the house wearing broad smiles on their faces.

'Granddad!' James called out, jogging forward. 'You made it.'

Wilmore smiled at him. 'Of course I made it,' he said. 'Why wouldn't I?'

Mary nodded. 'And he's early, too.'

Ben looked up at Wilmore. 'Can we leave right now?'

'Why?'

'The dishes still have to be done.'

Wilmore hesitated. 'Erm, sorry, Ben, I can't just up and leave. I'll have to speak with Anne Brown for a moment.'

Ben rolled his eyes. He had a feeling that Wilmore would say that.

'I think that's a very good idea,' said Brown, appearing at the front door, her arms folded.

After setting Mary on the ground, Wilmore looked up at the doorway. 'You must be Anne.'

'That's right.' Brown looked Wilmore up and down. 'I presume you're Mr Clyde?'

Wilmore moved forward, straightening the collar of his coat. 'Yes, I'm Wilmore. Nice to finally meet you, Anne.'

They shook hands and Brown said, in a very sharp voice, 'Likewise. I've heard quite a lot about you recently. Please, come in; there are some forms I need you to sign.'

'Of course,' replied Wilmore, turning and facing the children. 'Go and wait for me in the car. I won't be too long.'

Running across the garden, James managed to win the race for the passenger seat, while Ben had to be content with the backseat.

Mary, who was just happy to be leaving, climbed quietly into the back of the car.

Ben gave Mary a nudge. 'Quick, roll down your window,' he told her.

Mary narrowed her eyes. 'Why?'

'Er, to hear what they're saying,' said Ben.

'How could we hear that from here?' asked Mary, with a look of disgust.

'If they start shouting at one another, we will,' replied Ben.

Mary stared at him, her face angry. 'Just shut up!'

About five minutes later, Wilmore arrived at the car with a sheet of paper in his hand. When he got in, Ben leaned forward and said, 'Everything alright?'

Wilmore started the car. 'Everything's fine,' he replied. 'Just some formalities to sort out.'

As the car drove off, James looked across at his grandfather. He couldn't help thinking again of the bizarre story he had overheard the night before. He would have to pluck up the courage and ask his grandfather about it; that was the only logical step to take.

Drifting to sleep, James decided not to dwell on the matter. From now on, he would think positively. Mindful of this, one such thought popped into his head – he was spending Christmas with his grandfather.

CHAPTER EIGHT

Wilmore Clyde's House

He was woken by the ticking sound of the indicator. Stretching his arms, he wondered if he had been sleeping long. 'How long was I out for?'

'Not long,' replied Wilmore. 'Perfect timing, though – we're here.'

The car mounted a speed bump, causing a slight jolt that awoke Ben and Mary in the backseat.

Through the thick trees, the exterior of the house gradually came into view. It was quite a sight.

James knew the house was very old and dated as far back as the 13th century. Although recently refurbished, the mansion still held the appearance of a medieval castle, with its beautifully constructed stone walls towering high into the sky.

The sprawling estate also boasted two long gardens, complete with luxurious water fountains, and at the back of the house there were fields as lengthy as a golf course.

The car came to a stop before two black gates and James peered out the windscreen, taking everything in.

On either side of the gates were stone plinths on which sat two fearsome-looking eagles, their wings extended as though they were about to take off.

Taking a deep breath, Wilmore rolled down his windscreen and pressed several buttons on an electronic monitor, each one beeping as they were touched.

From the passenger seat, James could see that the first two buttons dialled in were seven and five, but after that, his eyes couldn't keep up with the speed of his grandfather's fingers. To pass the time and not to appear nosy, he looked out of the windscreen again.

Beside each plinth were two fully grown oak trees, their branches meeting and forming an archway over the entrance. They provided great shelter and the ground directly beneath them was the only area not covered in snow.

A moment later, after the monitor had accepted the password, the gates opened and the car coasted up the long, tree-lined driveway towards the house.

Suddenly, the garden lights were activated, displaying the house in greater detail.

Ivy shrouded the walls of the mansion and there were so many turrets and towers that James didn't know where to begin looking. He had always assumed his grandfather was a very wealthy man, but he had never dared to ask him.

Mary, not one to dodge questions, asked, 'Wilmore, are you rich?'

Wilmore chuckled. 'Not in the slightest.'

'But this house is huge,' Mary pointed out.

Wilmore turned to Mary. 'Actually, this house was given to me.'

'Given to you!' gasped Mary. 'By who?'

'A friend.'

Ben was grinning. 'I need new friends.'

'So, will I ever get to keep this house?' asked Mary.

'That's not likely,' Ben told her.

Mary shrugged. 'Why not?'

'You're a girl,' said Ben.

'You don't say!'

'Only a man can own this house.' Ben smiled at her. 'Oh, someone like me!'

'Excuse me, but I'm his grandson,' said James, joining the argument.

'And?' said Ben.

'And I would get the house,' replied James in a confident tone of voice.

'What would you do with it?' said Mary.

James looked and her and said, 'I would give it to you.'

Mary's face broke into a smile. 'See!'

Ben was frowning hard. 'It would never happen!'

Wilmore had to laugh. 'I'm glad we got that sorted out,' he said. 'Now then, shall we go inside?'

'Yes, please,' said Mary, getting out of the car.

Wilmore handed James the house keys. 'It's the first gold key.'

On the way to the front door, Ben lifted his hand over his head and shook a branch that lay directly over Mary, showering her with snow.

'Missed,' said Mary.

'No, I didn't,' replied Ben.

After walking up several stones steps, James, Wilmore and Ben reached the large oak door.

James started smiling to himself. Although he had seen this house many times before, he still always felt an overwhelming sense of excitement whenever he arrived.

As James opened the front door, Wilmore spoke to Mary. 'Come inside, sweetheart, or you'll catch your death.'

James pushed the heavy door open, feeling the warm breeze on his face.

'Careful,' said Wilmore, nodding at a steep step as he entered the house.

The children followed him inside, not yet able to see much as the lights were off and the only source of illumination was coming from the moon.

'I'm going to put you in a different room this year.' Wilmore dusted snow from his coat with one hand and used the other to flick on the lights. The vestibule lit up, revealing its grandeur.

James raised his eyes.

Overhead, hanging from the dome-shaped ceiling, was a crystal chandelier; old and elegant. Further down the hall, past the staircase, another chandelier hung; this one unlit.

Wilmore said jovially, 'Let there be light.'

'Are they safe?' said Ben, peering up at the chandeliers.

Wilmore turned, surprised. 'Safe?'

'Well,' said Ben, 'supposing one fell on you?'

Wilmore smiled. 'Well, I wouldn't fancy my chances if that happened, but not to worry – this house is strong and true.'

With the lights now on, the children could see the vestibule properly. Large red carpets shrouded the walls, lying over antique tables and chairs, giving the hall a regal look.

Gazing to the right of the vestibule, the children could see stone statues of large men standing in a line, all of whom were holding swords out before them. Around their waists were belts equipped with an assortment of dangerous weaponry.

Mary extended her right index finger and, moving it up the line of statues, started to count how many there were.

'12,' said Wilmore, watching Mary closely.

'Who are they?' asked James. 'They weren't here last year.'

'Isn't it obvious?' said Wilmore, unbuttoning his overcoat.

'They're men,' Ben observed cleverly.

Mary sighed and said, 'Well, of course they're men, but what men?'

Wilmore glanced over his shoulder suspiciously before inching closer to the children. 'They're knights,' he whispered.

'Knights?' said the children together.

Wilmore hung his overcoat on a clothes stand then said, 'From the stories. You're looking at the legendary 12 knights of Zara.'

Ben was still having trouble believing him. 'But they're just stories – fairytales.'

Wilmore shook his head. 'The stories are true.' He pointed to himself. 'I should know. I've been there.'

'You were in Orchestra?' said Ben.

Wilmore nodded, looking very serious. 'I lived there for most of my life. In Zara, I might add – not Darken.'

James eyed a glass cabinet at the far side of the hall displaying swords and other fearsome shaped blades that looked like props from a horror film. 'Is that where you got all those swords then?'

'Precisely.'

'But I don't see any magic diamonds,' said Mary. 'Where are they?'

Wilmore turned to face Mary. 'For generations, the diamonds remained hidden. Until recently, that is.'

'How many diamonds are there again?' asked Ben.

Mary raised her hand. 'Can I answer that?'

Wilmore smiled. 'Go ahead.'

'Three!'

'That's correct,' said Wilmore. 'Once all three are united, the possessor will be granted immortality.'

Mary frowned. 'What's that?'

'Everlasting life,' Wilmore told her.

Mary shook her head.

'You never die,' explained James, looking down at Mary.

The children gazed at Wilmore for a few seconds, wondering if he was serious.

From a coffee table beside the door, Wilmore lifted a candle stand and pointed it towards a lofty staircase in the middle of the hall. 'Shall we continue?' He walked forward, smiling. 'Follow me.'

A few minutes later, Wilmore stopped walking, pushed open a large oak door and guided the children into a high-ceilinged room. It was lit solely by a roaring fire and adorned with a newly cut and beautifully decorated Christmas tree.

Huge portraits of family members long since dead hung on the walls, and James noticed that the mantelpiece was emblazoned with holly and tinsel.

Letting his eyes wander, he also saw three elegant canopy beds, and at the far side of the room there were interconnecting doors to an outside balcony.

Mary looked up at Wilmore. 'So, where will I sleep?'

'Well, my dear, do you see the bed where the doll is lying?'

Mary took a quick look at each of the three beds and her eyes stopped on one with a beautiful porcelain doll tucked under the quilt. She pointed. 'Is it that one?'

Wilmore laughed. 'It is.'

Mary ran over to her bed, lay down and felt her back sinking into the mattress as if it were a sponge.

After James and Ben had chosen their beds, Wilmore moved towards them and said, 'Now, why don't you go outside and play for a while?'

James nodded. 'I suppose we could.'

Wilmore walked over to a dresser at the far side of the room, opened it and started rummaging around. 'Let's find you some warmer clothes.' He randomly picked three coats and set them down on Mary's bed.

Minutes later, when warmly clothed, the children ran outside into the misty December night, alternating their time between the field at the back of the house and the garden at the front.

Two hours had passed before they finally returned to their bedroom.

'Good night,' said Wilmore, ushering the children into their beds. 'We'll talk more in the morning after a good night's sleep.'

Before switching off the lights, Wilmore took one final look around the bedroom, only to jump suddenly when he saw Ben grasping a snowball in his hand and taking dead aim at Mary's head. 'Perhaps you should give me that, Ben,' he said quickly, holding out the large palm of his hand.

Annoyed by having been caught, Ben sighed and reluctantly handed the snowball over. Cursing his luck, he crept over to his bed.

'He would've missed anyway, Wilmore,' said Mary, glancing angrily over at Ben.

Fighting back a smile, Wilmore turned off the lights. 'Sweet dreams,' he said, his voice soft.

Then he left the room.

As soon as he had shut the door, the children sat up in their beds, listening to the footsteps of Wilmore diminishing down the corridor. Gradually, the patter of his shoes became more distant, until finally there were none at all.

All they could hear now, apart from their own excited breaths, was the grandfather clock ticking noisily outside the door.

Moments later, the ancient clock chimed for midnight and the children hurried from their warm beds.

James stepped out on to the balcony, from which he could see for miles in every direction. He felt like he had just opened a secret portal into another world.

Snow was falling steadily and the stars shone like diamonds in the sky. He gazed to his left, noticing the snow-covered rooftops that glistened under the silvery moonlight.

It was quite a sight – overwhelming, almost. He wanted to cherish every moment of his freedom. He sighed with contentment.

Whatever tomorrow had in store, it didn't matter. Tonight, he was free. After taking a deep breath, James Clyde savoured that thought. *Free.*

Then, closing his eyes and feeling the snow on his face, he wished the moment would never end.

- CHAPTER NINE -

The Mysterious Door

Later that night, James got out of bed and donned his blue bed robe. 'Let's be quick about this.'

'Sure.' Ben put on his glasses and kicked the blankets off. 'They're in the kitchen downstairs.'

'Where are you two going?' said Mary, sitting up.

Ben groaned. 'Don't tell me you're still awake.'

'Ben's hungry,' said James. 'We're going for biscuits.'

Mary looked up at James in expectancy. 'Can I come too?'

James flashed a smile. 'Let's go!'

Ben grabbed Mary by the arm. 'Stay close behind us, blondie. I don't want you getting lost.'

As quietly as he could, James tiptoed out of the door. Cautiously, he led the way as they travelled down the staircases, taking one step at a time, just in case any of them stumbled or made a sound that might awaken Wilmore.

The light of the moon beamed through the large dome-shaped windows, lighting their path as they crept past the sword cabinet, only then noticing the lifelike statues of the 12 knights of Zara.

The eyes of the statues seemed to be following James and watching every move he made. Crossing the creaky wooden floor, he made his way into the spacious kitchen, opening and closing the door as quietly as he could.

Ben pointed to a cabinet above the sink and whispered, 'It's that one. Quickly, get me a chair.'

'How do you know it's that one?' said Mary, as she opened the door slightly to peep out into the hall.

'I'm smarter than you, that's how.' Ben sighed. 'People, I need a chair, quickly!'

Ever so quietly, James carried a chair over to Ben, who jumped up on to it and pulled the cabinet open. As expected, right next to the tea bags was an unopened tin of biscuits.

James was smiling. For as long as he could remember, his grandfather had been hiding the biscuits in the same place.

Suddenly, the door through which they had entered slammed shut, creating a gunshot-like sound. If that hadn't awoken Wilmore, nothing would.

Grimacing, James opened the door again and waved Mary out. 'C'mon, we'd better get out of here before we're caught.'

'Let's just take the whole tin,' said Ben, jumping down from the chair before placing it back under the kitchen table.

Mary sighed. 'That's really smart, Ben,' she said sarcastically. 'Wilmore would never notice it gone.'

'Right, leave the tin and let's get out of here,' said James.

The children walked quickly from the kitchen and crept soundlessly up the giant staircase, holding on to the banister as they went. They reached the top of the stairs, but instead of travelling back to their room, they ventured up another level in the house, eager to find unexplored territory.

The next corridor they passed was dimly lit by hanging lamps and resembled an art gallery in a museum. It was truly magnificent. Both sides of the walls were covered in beautifully painted frescos.

James walked along, glancing at each work of art as he passed. Then one caught his eye. He couldn't miss this painting as it took centre stage over the rest.

It was positioned on its own in the middle of the wall, enclosed in a gold frame, and looked stunning in the faint light. He moved closer and inspected the masterpiece, running the tips of his fingers on the smooth canvas. Above the frame, engraved into a gold plaque, was the word BETRAYAL.

The painting depicted two men sitting in an old wooden boat, gazing at a beautiful green diamond that seemed out of place in such a simple mode of transport. It was set at night, with three moons rather than one lighting the sky.

The men in the boat were dressed in long robes, one in blue, the other in black, and they looked totally in awe of this sparkling diamond.

The man in the blue robe was elderly, with a long white beard that resembled candyfloss. His hands were cupped, handling the marvellous diamond with the greatest of care, like a father holding his newborn baby for the first time.

The other man looked more mysterious, with a hood and cowl that partially covered his face, but James could still see the glint in the hooded man's eyes.

It looked as though the men were almost afraid of the diamond, worshipping it as they travelled along the water.

James's gaze switched from one man to the other, wondering which of them had committed the terrible act of betrayal.

The painting, he knew, had to be set in Orchestra; the land his grandfather had always told him so much about. The jewel in the elderly man's hands had to be one of the magical and mysterious diamonds that were supposedly buried in this land.

'We should keep going,' said Ben, laying a hand on James's shoulder.

James jumped; he felt hypnotised by the painting, as if the diamond was somehow using its power to lure him in. The more he looked at the painting, the more fascinated he became. But Ben was right – they should keep moving.

James nodded, touched the texture of the painting one last time and followed Ben and Mary along the corridor, towards another part of the house.

When they had rounded a few more corners, they came to

another long stretch of corridor, this one slightly different than the rest, with a rickety old rocking chair sitting against the wall, as if an invisible man was keeping watch on this section of the house.

The chair began to rock back and forth gently as the children walked past, at which point James spotted something that struck him as strange. There were no doors or windows along this corridor. There were two narrow walls, a rocking chair and a red-carpeted floor.

That was it.

No rooms whatsoever. It was as if this corridor had been forgotten about; hidden from the rest of the house.

Then, all of a sudden, the corridor was illuminated with jets of gold light.

'What's going on?' shouted Ben, shielding his glasses. 'If this is some sort of a joke, James, it's not funny.'

Hands covering his eyes, James cried, 'Don't be stupid, Ben, I'm right beside you. How could I be doing anything?'

A moment later, the lights died and the children took their hands away from their eyes. They stared at the source of the brightness.

It was a door.

Strangely, unlike other wings of the house, this door stood all alone at the very end of the corridor, as though it were a secret portal to another world.

Suddenly, the lights returned, brighter than before. It looked as though somebody had switched a light on from inside the room, and yet the glow radiating around the corridor had to be coming from a stronger source than a lightbulb.

Then they dimmed again.

James, as always, was intrigued. He'd never seen anything like this before in the house. 'We need a volunteer.'

Mary rubbed her eyes and looked at James. 'To do what?'

'To open the door.'

'Count me out,' said Ben, squinting. 'My eyesight's even worse than usual right now!'

James thought that, being the eldest, he should take responsibility. He began to walk forward. 'Stay behind me.'

When close enough to the door, he could see that there were holes and broken wood on the surface, which explained how the strong beams were getting through, but didn't explain what actually lay behind the threshold.

Spurred on by Ben, James wrapped his hand around the handle of the door and turned it. 'It's locked!' he cried in disappointment.

'I knew it,' said Ben, throwing his arms in the air.

'Listen,' said James, trying to hide his disappointment, 'we can always try tomorrow night.'

'But what if it's locked then, too?' said Mary, as she made her way back along the corridor.

James turned to Mary and met her gaze with a wink. 'Trust me, Mary, it will open.'

- CHAPTER TEN -

The Man In Black

James slept late the next morning. Indeed, were it not for two knocks on the door, he might've slept later still.

Rubbing his eyes, he sat up in bed. 'Come in.'

The door swung open and his grandfather came strolling into the room carrying a silver tray, upon which sat three glasses of orange juice. 'Good morning.'

'It's the morning?' said James with a heavy yawn, looking around the gloomy room. 'It looks more like the middle of the night.'

Wilmore crossed the room and pulled open the drapes. Standing before the long window, holding the tray in both hands, he looked out at the snowy countryside. 'And don't expect the day to get any brighter, either.'

'Why's that?'

'It's the shortest day of the year,' Wilmore pointed out, taking a glass of juice from the tray and handing it to James.

James took a sip of his juice. 'Thanks.'

'There's been more snow,' said Wilmore.

'Really?'

Wilmore nodded. 'Maybe two more inches have fallen over the course of the night.'

'Oi, Ben,' shouted James, 'did you hear that? More snow!'

Ben mumbled something back before pulling the blankets up over his head.

'I'll tell him later,' said James, smiling up at his grandfather.

Wilmore sat down on the bed. 'Listen, James, I've got to go into town for a little while. I would prefer it if you all stayed in the house.'

James drained his glass, then wiped his mouth. 'No problem.'

Wilmore shifted nervously on the bed. 'Please don't venture outside for even a moment until I come back. Is that clear?'

James hadn't noticed it until now, but his grandfather looked absolutely dreadful. There was perspiration on his brow and dark shadows under his eyes, as if he had stayed up all night with worry.

Wilmore went on, 'If somebody comes to the house and knocks on the door, you ignore it. If the phone rings, you don't answer it.'

James nodded, a little worried now. 'Granddad, is everything alright?'

Wilmore forced a smile. 'Everything's fine,' he said. 'Try and get some rest.' He got up from the bed and walked towards the door, then turned back to James. 'I shouldn't be too long.'

Then, shutting the door behind him, Wilmore Clyde left the room.

★

Having dressed himself and applied his hair gel, James stood before a long oval-shaped window on the fourth storey, watching as his grandfather drove out the gates of the house. The car turned left and slowly out of sight.

Hanging his head, James sat down beside the window and heaved a frustrated sigh. Perhaps his grandfather was in financial trouble. Whatever the reason, there was definitely something wrong.

Looking out the window again, James saw something that surprised him. Far below, there seemed to be a menacing dark presence standing inside the grounds of the house. Thinking that he was seeing things, he rubbed his eyes and looked again.

An oblique black line still remained. From such a distance, it looked as though a dark demon was lingering by the gates. It appeared very much like someone had waited for the gates to open and entered the premises.

'Ben,' called James.

'What?'

'Come here and see this.'

'See what?'

'Just come here!'

Ben appeared at the door of his bedroom, still dressed in his pyjamas. 'Huh? See what, exactly?'

James groaned and went towards Ben. 'Just come here, will you?' He pushed Ben forward. 'Take a look out there.'

Ben peered out the window, then back at James. 'It must've snowed heavily last night.'

James shook his head and stared out the window, but no matter how much he wanted to see the dark figure, he had to admit that whatever had been there wasn't now.

'What's wrong?' said Ben.

James rubbed his eyes. 'Nothing. I'm imagining things now.'

Ben smiled. 'Well, go downstairs and imagine me up some breakfast.'

'Yes sir!' said James sarcastically, heading downstairs, making his way into the scullery on the second storey. There, he found three bowls of cereal and a jug of milk already prepared on a tray.

After finishing his cereal, he lifted the tray and returned to his room, finding Ben and Mary running around outside in the corridor, hitting each other with large snowballs.

Mary ran over to the window. 'C'mon, let's go outside.'

James frowned at her. 'Not just yet. Wilmore's gone into town and I promised him we'd stay inside until he comes back.'

'Oops. You probably should've told us that a few minutes ago,' said Ben, pointing down at his feet.

Looking down, James noticed Ben was wearing Wilmore's old

hiking boots. There were lumps of snow around the floor and small puddles had started to form. 'That's just great.'

Mary pointed out the window. 'There's a scary man at the gates,' she said suddenly.

'Nah, there's not,' James told her. 'It's just the shadow of the trees. I thought I saw somebody earlier as well.'

'It is a man,' insisted Mary. 'He keeps coming and going.'

Placing the tray on the floor, James went over to the window. He stood for a long moment, concentrating on the gates. For a split second, he thought Mary had been mistaken, just as he had been minutes earlier.

Until…

As he looked closer, a black speck appeared in the distance. Then the speck turned into a shadow, and then, finally, the silhouette became a man.

The stranger's long coat was black, as black as coal. His trousers were also black, as were his shirt and tie.

Ben hoisted himself up on James's shoulders, trying to catch a better look. 'Who's that, then?'

'Isn't it obvious?' said James.

'Nope,' said Ben after a moment.

James's face wore a broad smile. 'He's the man in black.'

CHAPTER ELEVEN

Don't Let Him In!

Despite the obvious beauty of Wilmore Clyde's stately mansion, there were times when James felt the house was a little spooky.

Even the faintest sounds tended to be exaggerated. For example, if the wind howled outside, it would give the impression that people were whispering around the dark corridors. If somebody tiptoed across the creaky wooden floor on the third storey, this would be heard in every corner of the second.

So it came as no surprise to James that the constant knocking on the front door echoed to where they now stood, on the fourth storey.

James shook his head and looked Ben straight in the eye. 'Don't answer it.'

'Why not?' said Ben. 'It's only the postman.'

'That's no postman,' said James, nodding at the window.

'Postmen don't wear long black coats,' added Mary.

Ben looked at Mary, then James, then back at Mary. 'They do if it's cold. What's wrong with you two? You're getting me nervous now.'

And then the knocking stopped.

'See,' Ben whispered, 'he's leaving.'

James craned his neck and looked down at the long driveway, but there was no sign of the man. 'Why hasn't he left, then?'

'Maybe he's writing a note.' Ben nodded. 'Then he's going to slip it under the door.'

James shrugged. 'I suppose he could be.'

The words had barely left James's mouth when he heard the sound of the front door banging shut far below.

The air grew colder, as if the door had been lying open for some time.

'What was that?' said Mary, looking anxiously over at James.

James suddenly had a sinking feeling. 'He's in the house!' He shot Ben a sharp look. 'You forgot to lock the door again, didn't you?'

Ben shrugged. 'I didn't know it had to be locked!'

James pulled Mary towards him. 'Quick, this way – let's get to the highest part of the house.'

CHAPTER TWELVE

No Way Out

James, with Mary holding his hand tightly, ran as fast as he possibly could down the long dark corridor, passing by the many suits of armour lining both walls. He found the last door at the very end of the corridor and rushed inside.

Sticking his head out the frame of the door, he looked in all directions, trying to make out any unusual shadows. Frowning hard, he saw nothing but darkness.

'Please tell me he's not out there,' whispered Ben, removing his glasses, trying to control his excessive blinking.

James went back into the room. 'No sign! How long should we stay in here?'

'Up to you,' replied Ben, walking further into the room, which looked more like a library, with the walls dominated by huge bookcases.

James's eyes were lingering on the floor, tracking Ben's movements around the room. He could hardly believe what he was seeing. There was still a large amount of snow on the heels of Ben's boots and they were leaving a watery trail.

'Ben, you idiot,' cried Mary.

Ben turned and looked at her. 'What's wrong now?' he asked apprehensively.

James spoke first. 'You've left a trail.'

It was then that they heard distant footsteps.

Quickly, James looked out the door and caught a glimpse of a long black shadow at the head of the corridor. With a frown, he closed the door and took two steps back. 'I think we've a problem.'

'He's coming, isn't he?' said Mary in a worried voice.

James nodded sheepishly. 'Somebody's out there! We have to do something, quick.'

'Like what?' whispered Ben. 'He's already outside in the corridor, for goodness' sake. We can't run for it now.'

James looked around the room. There was absolutely nowhere to hide. 'We can't just wait here,' he whispered back. 'We have to try and run for it.'

But it was too late.

All eyes turned to the door as it began to creak open. A silhouette formed in the threshold.

James took Mary's hand and held it tightly, watching as the figure at the door slowly materialised.

- CHAPTER THIRTEEN -

A Strange Man Came to the House

Mary heaved a sigh. 'Wilmore, you frightened us.'

Wilmore shook his head. 'I forgot this,' he said, waving his wallet in the air. 'I thought I made myself perfectly clear. I specifically asked you not to go outside, but I arrived home to find the front door lying open.'

'It was all Mary's idea,' said Ben, pointing to his sister.

'No, it wasn't.'

Ben shrugged. 'Well it wasn't mine, blondie.'

'Stop blaming me!' cried Mary.

Wilmore held his hand aloft, an act that silenced the children immediately. 'Well, I suppose I can't blame you for being curious about the house, but I would prefer to know where you go. Now, please return to your room.'

'Now look what you've done, Mary,' said Ben with a deep sigh.

'That's quite enough.' Wilmore lifted Mary over to the door. 'Do you think you can find your way back?'

Mary nodded confidently. 'You should stay with Ben, though,' she said. 'He couldn't find his way out of this room.'

'Very funny.'

Without another word, Mary ran down the corridor and rounded the corner.

Turning and facing James and Ben, Wilmore raised his grey eyebrows. 'I have to say I'm disappointed. I expected better here. I have to be able to leave you alone from time to time.'

'I'm sorry,' said James. 'I went downstairs and when I came back, they had already been outside.'

Ben hung his head. 'I'm sorry. I had no idea we weren't allowed outside.'

Wilmore nodded and his features softened. 'Yes, well, let's not dwell on it.' From his coat pocket, he took out a white envelope sealed with red wax and waved it in the air. 'This was sitting on the coffee table when I came in. Did you see who left this?'

James nodded. 'There was a man here.'

Wilmore narrowed his eyes. 'What man?'

'The man in black!' cried Ben, taking off his glasses and waving them in the air for dramatic effect.

Wilmore rolled his eyes. 'And who exactly would that be?'

James gave Ben a funny look. 'A man dressed in black came to the house.'

'You didn't speak to him, did you?' said Wilmore.

James shook his head. 'No. We came up here because we thought he was in the house.'

Wilmore nodded, looking worried.

'Why?' said Ben. 'Who is he?'

Wilmore forced a smile. 'Probably just the postman.'

Ben nudged James in the ribs. 'See!'

Holding the door open, Wilmore said, 'I'll be along shortly. Please go straight back to your room.'

James and Ben did as they were asked.

★

Wilmore, meanwhile, opened the envelope, unfolded the note, and began to read.

- CHAPTER FOURTEEN -

The Letter

$\mathcal{D}$ear Wilmore,

$\mathcal{Y}$our presence is requested in the main street of the next town on the 21st of December. As the letter would suggest, I know where you live. Please understand you have no other option left, so I beg you to co-operate. This is your last chance to do the right thing. 12 midnight. Bring the diamond, come alone and perhaps this can be resolved peacefully.

$\mathcal{K}$indest personal regards,

$\mathcal{G}$ilbert

Wilmore let the letter drop to the floor. The words he had read shocked him.

He would have to formulate a plan and get himself ready for what lay ahead, but it wouldn't be easy.

Killing someone, after all, never was.

CHAPTER FIFTEEN

The Sacred Secret

The remainder of the day seemed to pass somewhat slowly. Usually, James would find no end of things to do in the house, but given the events of the day already, he felt it was best not to stray too far from his bedroom.

It was the darkest day he had ever seen. The sun never broke through and the grey clouds seemed full of snow not yet fallen.

Dinner was held at 3 P.M. inside the enormous dining room on the second storey.

A long oak table with benches instead of chairs ran the entire length of the room, and James half expected a crowd of people to come walking through the door at any moment to join them.

In the evening, tea was served in the first storey banquet hall – the one room that James had come to know better than any other during his time in the house.

After a tour of the house, taking in the enormous library, the great hall and the many tapestries, the children retired to their bedroom.

Now, in his room, James went out on to the balcony and rested his arms on the railing, looking out across the sprawling estate.

Strangely, the night seemed brighter than the day. There was a crescent moon and a multitude of stars dotted the sky. A mixture of calmness and well-being came over him. The incident that happened earlier seemed a long time ago now. He had never felt happier.

Or safer.

★

Three storeys below, inside his lush personal quarters, Wilmore Clyde stood silently before a large painting, which hung on a wall nearest the door. A sweat had broken across his forehead and it had nothing to do with the many staircases he had just descended.

The moonlight shone through two large windows, revealing a few items of furniture: a sword cabinet, a grandfather clock and a round desk on which lay a flashlight and several letters, each one piled on top of the other.

Taking a deep breath, he lifted the painting by its gold frame and propped it against the door. Doing his best to remain calm, he went over to the desk and returned with the flashlight. Switching it on, he pointed the beam through the opening where the painting had once hung.

Through the cobwebs, he could see a dark green safety deposit box. As he twisted the lock three places to the right, he felt a large spider scurry across his knuckles.

Trembling, he refocused on the task at hand. He was close now. *So very close.* Ever so quickly, he moved the dial back one place to the left. The lock opened with a loud click.

Slowly, but confidently, he raised his hand and opened the door.

At once, the room exploded with light.

Green light.

Light so bright that Wilmore thought his vision would never fully recover. His hands shielding his face, he looked away.

A moment later, sensing the lights had died, he turned his eyes back to the deposit box. Heart pounding, he dropped to his knees in reverence and pressed a hand over his mouth, transfixed.

It was beautiful, too magnificent for words. Gently, carefully, he moved his hand towards the red cushion upon which it sat. Then he stopped. *Not yet*, he thought, closing and locking the deposit box. *Not just yet!*

At that moment, the grandfather clock began to chime. He turned, startled. 11P.M. It had been 11 long years since he had last killed. He looked towards the sword cabinet, his eyes searching for the sharpest weapon.

His next killing, he knew, was now just one hour away.

CHAPTER SIXTEEN

The Mysterious Door Opens

From the comfort of his warm bed, James was sitting up and watching the last flame in the fire fighting to stay alive. At last the orange flame minimised and died, a ribbon of smoke swirling off to the side.

He looked across at Mary, who was sleeping soundly with her arms wrapped lovingly around her doll.

Ben, however, was tossing and turning, frustrated at his inability to sleep. 'I'm bored,' he muttered, putting on his glasses. He squinted over at James. 'I know you're still awake, too.'

James rolled his eyes. 'Who, me?'

'Yes, you!'

'No I'm not!'

Ben sighed deeply. 'Wise guy, huh? Let's check the "you know what"!'

James was thinking the exact same thing. 'Okay.' He kicked off the bed covers, put one hand out for his bed robe, the other locating his slippers by the side of the bed.

Suddenly, there was a loud thud, followed by a high-pitched squeal. Donning his blue robe, James walked across the room and looked at Ben, who was rubbing his knee and cursing under his breath.

James put a finger to his lips. 'Be quiet,' he said, keeping his voice low. 'Mary's still asleep!'

Tears were welling in Ben's eyes. 'Sorry.'

'Look, over there.' James grabbed Ben by the arm and pointed to the far side of the room, where there was a table, on which stood a candle stand.

Ben winked. 'Leave it to me,' he whispered. Soundlessly, he crossed the room, glancing at Mary's bed as he went.

When he reached the table, he picked up a box of matches which lay just beside the stand. He swiped a match over the brown strip on the side of the box and a flame ignited, casting a glow to all corners of the room. He lit the candle, blew the match out and set it on the table.

Turning around, he suddenly noticed everywhere still appeared dark. The sudden explosion of light and the billowing smoke from the tip of the candle were combining to blind him. *James?*'

'Psst! Over here.'

'Huh?'

'I'm over here.'

Ben could see nothing. 'Where?' A shadow closed in on him.

'C'mon,' said James, pulling Ben towards the door.

'Is that you, James?' asked Ben, still dazed.

James sighed. 'Well, who else do you think it is?'

Ben held the candle far away from his face, trying to regain his sight. He was bumping into things and generally making noise.

'Why don't you just wake Mary up and tell her we're about to search the house?' said James as sarcastically as he could.

'Shut up!' snapped Ben, adjusting his glasses. 'It's these things. My eyesight seems to be getting worse.'

James frowned. 'Sorry. Let's just go.'

Holding the guttering candle out before him, Ben opened the door and waved his free hand forward, inviting James out into the hallway first.

Smiling and putting the previous disagreement behind him, James moved out into the hallway and, turning back, made sure Ben closed the door quietly. Then, walking side by side, they advanced further along the corridor, glancing at the numerous doors on either side of them.

Although, apart from Wilmore, they were the only people who lived in this house, all the doors were closed and locked, as if hundreds of people were staying over this Christmas.

Using his left hand, Ben checked if any of the doors were open, but they were all locked. Still, it didn't really matter: the only door that did matter was the one they were gradually moving towards.

Quickly, they continued on their way, hoping they were going in the right direction.

The long, winding corridors reminded James of a labyrinth: once you rounded a few corners, you would be doing well to find your way back.

After several more complicated twists and turns, James and Ben stopped prematurely and stood still with wide smiles on their faces.

They now knew that if their calculations were correct, and assuming they hadn't taken any wrong turns, then the mysterious door would be just around the next corner.

Turning the corner, they discovered the familiar rocking chair and the long stretch of corridor. However, they still couldn't see the door, but they knew it had to be there, for they had definitely been here before.

Suddenly, the dark corridor became very bright, revealing the door. Jets of yellow light beamed from every crevice, as if the door was somehow aware of their presence.

James smiled and, showing no fear, he began to walk along the red-carpeted floor.

Ben held out a trembling hand and muttered, 'I don't think this is such a good idea. Let's go back to the room.' He tried his best to feign a yawn. 'Look at that. I reckon I'll be able to sleep now.'

James rolled his eyes. 'Are you crazy? We've already come this far.'

Ben stuttered a response. 'I… I suppose we could go a little further.' He hesitated, nodding at the door. 'Has it ever occurred to you that maybe we're not supposed to know what's behind the door?'

James was shaking his head. 'But –'

'If I had to take a guess,' Ben went on, 'I'd say it's locked for a very good reason.'

'Yeah, I know,' said James, 'but I want to find that *reason* out!'

'Oh have it your way,' said Ben after a long pause, waving a hand forward.

Accepting the invitation, James crept along the corridor, followed by Ben, the candle shaking furiously in his right hand.

Shivering with anticipation, James stopped just yards before the door. *What secrets do you hide?*

'Pointless,' said Ben. 'It's going to be locked.'

'There's only one way to find out.' With his eyes closed, James tried to open the door, but as he did this, the handle began to shake. The door trembled fiercely, as if somebody was on the other side, trying to prevent him from entering.

'Let's get out of here, James,' cried Ben. 'This house is haunted.'

Feeling unsure, James pulled his hand away and the lights died; the trembling also stopped.

'C'mon,' said Ben, turning to leave. 'Whatever is behind that door doesn't want us getting inside.'

James stood his ground. He couldn't possibly leave now.

Ben, frowning, cried, 'James!'

'What?'

'Let's get out of here.'

'No!'

'What?'

'NO!'

Before Ben could protest, James grabbed the handle, turned it, and to his surprise, the door started to push open. He had to shove quite hard now as the door seemed to be stiff from disuse. It was like pushing against a brick wall. But it was definitely opening.

Eventually, he had it open far enough to be able to walk through. 'Where did all the lights go?'

Knees shaking with fear, Ben looked around. 'I have no idea.' Then he fumbled around the walls, trying to find a light switch, but couldn't come across one. He shrugged at James, who sighed and said, 'Give me that stand.'

Ben passed the candle stand over, delighted to finally part ways with it, just in case he saw something he didn't wish to.

Slowly, James moved around the room, holding the candle out before him.

'The room is empty,' said Ben, 'but I could've sworn –'

'It's not empty,' said James, shining the stand towards the corner of the room, where a large chest sat pressed against the wall. It was big and brown with marvellous gold trimmings around the edges. In the middle hung a gold padlock the size of a pear. It looked like a treasure chest, as though it had been stolen from a pirate ship.

Like two statues, James and Ben stood still, staring at the mysterious chest.

'James, it's got gold inside,' cried Ben excitedly.

James frowned. A seed of doubt slowly settled in his mind. Was his grandfather hiding something inside this chest?

After glancing at one another, James and Ben hurried over to the chest, slid on to their knees and tried to open it, but they couldn't.

James ran his fingertips over the slightly jagged surface of the chest, like a detective trying to find a hidden clue. The treasure chest, however, was locked securely. 'Check for a key,' he ordered, pulling at the padlock with one hand, while the other signalled Ben to search around the room.

All of a sudden, they heard faint footsteps approaching. They ducked behind the treasure chest, only then realising that the footsteps were getting louder and closer.

They froze.

'See, I knew we should've turned back,' whispered Ben, giving James a nudge. The hinges creaked as the door swung open and a shadow appeared, large at first, then got smaller and smaller.

James and Ben swapped nervous looks as the candle flickered in the wind and went out.

'What are you doing in here?' said an angry voice.

Ben recognised it immediately and said, in a rather gruff voice, 'Mary, what are you doing out of bed?'

'Following you two,' she replied pointedly. 'If Wilmore finds us out of bed, he won't be very happy.'

'Okay, we'd better head back,' said James. As quickly as he could, he took Mary by the hand and led the way from the room.

Creeping back along the corridor, he gave Ben a nervous look. 'Let's try and make it back to our room without making any noise in case he catches us.'

★

One mile away, Wilmore Clyde reached town and parked his car beside a curb, where he could make a swift getaway if the situation called for it. He had just stepped from the driver's seat when his eyes fell on the enormous moon, which lit the entire street like floodlights on a football pitch. He checked his wrist watch under the moonlight: 11.45 P.M.

It would soon be the appointed time.

CHAPTER SEVENTEEN

Meeting Gilbert

The town looked magical and Wilmore couldn't help noticing the hum of excitement in the air. It was Christmas season and a large number of people were still taking advantage of the late night shopping.

In the town's square, a small assemblage of Christmas carollers were completing their hymn programme with a rendition of "Silent Night". They looked very happy and content, singing loudly as they warmed themselves beside a giant brazier.

Further down, a group of middle-aged women moved towards their cars, armed with shopping bags and moaning loudly about the weather, which they thought was the coldest they had ever experienced in their entire lives.

As the women said their goodbyes and drove off, Wilmore stood still, watching people gradually go their separate ways.

The final members of the carollers wished one another a happy Christmas, packed up their instruments and walked down the cobbled street, glancing inside every shop window as they reluctantly parted.

When their voices had diminished, Wilmore stood alone in the empty town. He looked around, his eyes suspicious of anything that moved in the breeze. He was watching closely for a shadow to appear and listening intently for the sound of crunching footsteps in the snow.

But there were none.

Although the shops were now closed, the lights in their windows remained on, displaying the Christmas trees and decorations. He walked across the street to a boutique shop and leaned his back against the red Georgian door.

Glancing into the shop window, he focused not on the clothes but on his reflection. His insides were churning, but outwardly he looked strong and confident; a throwback to the man he had been 11 years earlier.

Sucking in the cold air, he buttoned his overcoat up to his mouth and warmed his hands with his breath.

At that moment in an old, derelict church, the large bell tolled midnight and he jumped, startled by the thunderous noise. He covered his ears and moved from the doorway to the street, looking up at the church behind the shops. The hour had arrived, but there still wasn't a stir.

Two minutes went by.

Five.

Impatient, he paced towards the centre of the street, glancing left and right. 'Gilbert!' he called out. 'Show yourself!'

The wind suddenly picked up, sending a sheet of a discarded newspaper swirling into the air. A dark shadow formed some yards behind it.

Then a figure emerged.

For a long tense moment, neither man spoke. They just stood yards apart, like two gunslingers preparing for a quick draw.

The man before Wilmore's eyes was clad in black, moustachioed and the few remaining strands of hair on his head were slicked back.

Wilmore couldn't believe how little his former friend had changed.

The man in black moved further into the moonlight, slowly revealing a pistol clutched in his hand.

Wilmore took a step back in surprise. 'I thought you wanted to resolve this peacefully?'

'I do.'

'Then why the gun?'

'It's pretty straightforward, my good man.' Gilbert levelled the pistol at Wilmore. 'If you brought the diamond, you will live.'

'And if I didn't, then I'll die, right?' said Wilmore with a calm smile.

'You catch on quickly.'

Wilmore heard the pistol click.

Gilbert advanced, one hand holding the pistol, the other cupped and reaching forward. 'The diamond. Give it to me!'

CHAPTER EIGHTEEN

Tonight, It Ends

James Clyde still couldn't sleep. Feeling strangely anxious, he sat up in bed and looked around. Centuries-old antiques emblazoned the walls, but the room was now a lot colder – the fire had long since died and only the embers remained.

Throwing off the bed covers, he went across the room towards the balcony. Walking outside, he couldn't believe how cold it had become.

The snow had stopped and a severe frost had developed across the distant hills. Standing there, enjoying the view, he suddenly felt his hand being held. He looked down and saw Mary smiling broadly back.

James smiled. 'Can't you sleep either?'

'Ben won't stop snoring,' replied Mary, resting her arms on the snow-coated railing.

James let out a laugh. 'Oh, right. It can be a problem sometimes.'

'It's freezing out here,' said Mary, watching her breath leave like smoke from her lips.

'C'mon,' said James, taking Mary's hand, 'we'll go back inside. Do you reckon you'll be able to sleep now?'

Though it was late, Mary still felt wide awake. 'Nope. Can we stay out here just a little longer?'

James looked at her. 'Are you sure?'

Mary nodded. 'Do you want to go exploring again?' she suggested.

Frowning, James said, 'I don't think that's such a good idea.'

'In case your granddad catches us?'

'Well, it wouldn't be right to wake him,' James told her.

Mary wasn't convinced. 'Wilmore's fast asleep by now.'

★

In the next town, Wilmore Clyde stood perfectly still, peering down the barrel of a gun. 'The diamonds don't exist,' he cried, holding his hands in the air. 'You're chasing a figment of your imagination.'

'And yet you meet me,' Gilbert sneered.

'I had little choice,' replied Wilmore. 'You've come for James, haven't you?'

A thin smile crossed Gilbert's face. 'Ah yes, the last great hope for Orchestra.' He lowered his gun. 'I had almost forgotten about him.'

'Somehow, I doubt that,' said Wilmore with a shake of his head. 'You would really kill an innocent child?'

'I am here for the diamond, Wilmore – not the boy,' insisted Gilbert.

'And what about your queen? I find it hard to believe that she would just allow James to walk free.'

'That's true,' said Gilbert, nodding. 'Abigail is obsessed with the prophecies. I'll have to tell her something.'

Wilmore shrugged and said, 'Tell her you couldn't find him.'

Gilbert laughed jeeringly. 'We both know she wouldn't buy that.'

'Then I'm afraid we're at an impasse,' said Wilmore robustly.

'On the contrary, Wilmore. I have a solution.' Gilbert raised the pistol once more. 'One even *you* might find acceptable.'

Wilmore nodded to the outstretched pistol. 'Shooting me won't get you anywhere.'

'Perhaps not, but it's time for you to do the right thing,' said Gilbert. 'Hand the diamond over and I swear to you that no harm will befall the boy. I don't wish to spend any more time than is necessary in this world. I'll turn and leave.'

'I have your word on that?'

'You do.'

'And what's that worth? The word of a traitor?'

The pistol clicked loudly, echoing around the town. 'You forget, my friend, that you have very few options left. This war ends tonight.'

Wilmore closed his eyes and nodded. 'I agree.' Stealthily, he reached a hand behind his coat and grasped the hilt of his sword. 'Tonight, it ends.'

CHAPTER NINETEEN

The Attack

Wilmore's initial hopes over Gilbert's promises had quickly vanished, leaving him with a sense of inevitability. It was becoming increasingly clear that this meeting would not be ending in a truce. He felt Gilbert's gaze upon him.

'Your decision. The diamond or the boy?'

After a tense moment of silence, Wilmore took two paces forward. 'Return to Orchestra,' he said, as Gilbert's head dropped. 'I wish you luck finding the diamonds and offer a little advice: get bigger shovels and continue digging.'

Gilbert shook his head. 'I'm sorry you feel that way,' he said. 'I truly am. I never wanted it to end like this.' He levelled the pistol directly at Wilmore's midriff.

Wilmore glared at his former friend. 'Now it's time for *you* to do the right thing,' he cried. 'You used to be a knight. Please, it's not too late for you, Gilbert. Redeem yourself tonight.'

'It's gone too far.'

'Put the gun down,' said Wilmore, taking a step forward. 'We both know you're not going to shoot me.'

Gilbert looked up at the December sky, then back at Wilmore. 'Well spoken. I couldn't harm you – and I won't have to.'

Wilmore doubted that this was good news.

'Goodbye, Wilmore.' Pocketing the pistol, Gilbert turned and walked down the street, his shoes crunching on the snow. The sounds faded slowly and, moments later, stopped completely.

Wilmore refused to believe it was all over; it was too simple. His eyes scanned the entire town nervously.

All was calm.

Perhaps it was all over.

Then, out of the corner of his eye, he glimpsed a dark presence standing only yards away to his right. It wasn't Gilbert, for the shadowy form was at least five inches taller.

Instinctively, his hand fumbled for his sword, but it was too late.

A sword was inside Wilmore's stomach. Groaning in pain, he peered upwards. The red eyes glaring back were fearsome and full of cruelty.

Brutal cruelty.

- CHAPTER TWENTY -

Dakotas

The oversized red eyes seemed to dilate, as if the creature was somehow deriving pleasure from the act of killing. Wilmore screamed as the blade retracted.

Blood poured; the pain doubled.

Summoning strength from within, he brandished his sword and guided it into his assailant. The red eyes turned white and the creature dropped at his feet.

Two more creatures ran forward.

Showing no pity, he spun and flashed his great sword twice, killing the creatures in quick succession. Sensing another presence, he turned and parried a sword with a quick trust of his own blade.

At the same time, however, a powerful blow struck the back of his neck, sending him to his knees.

He tried to stand, but blows were raining in on him from every angle. He finally succumbed, falling to the snow with a dull thud.

The last image he saw, before he drifted into unconsciousness, were the murderous red eyes of a creature standing over him. It was a creature he knew well; a creature that still haunted his dreams.

A creature called a Dakota.

- CHAPTER TWENTY-ONE -

The Race

Slowly, as if awakening from a deep sleep, Wilmore Clyde's eyes opened. His head ached, but pain was good – pain told him he was still alive.

Groggy, he knelt on the ground, trying to recover, trying to regain his breath. His condition had worsened. It was as if some poisonous snake had bitten him and the deadly venom was gradually making its way into his bloodstream, killing him slowly from within.

Using the tip of his sword, he cut the sleeve off his coat and tied it around his stomach, staunching the bleeding.

He looked anxiously at his watch: 12.45 A.M. There was still time. Standing up, he briefly wondered why the creatures hadn't killed him. Perhaps they thought he was already dead.

Whatever the reason, he was grateful for the second chance. He thought of James. With the benefit of hindsight, he now realised he should've got the children out of the house.

Feeling a pang of regret, he stumbled towards his car and groaned as he got inside. Wincing, he turned the key in the ignition and the car started with a powerful roar. He hit the accelerator and, tires squealing, gunned the car down the street.

He knew every second mattered; he understood now that he was in a race where there would only be one winner.

Peering out the windscreen, steering the car around a dangerous bend, Wilmore Clyde said a silent prayer, hoping that the victor would be him.

- CHAPTER TWENTY-TWO -

Intruder Alert!

James and Mary were walking through the balcony doors when Ben came rushing over to them, looking agitated.

Mary felt a vague displeasure at seeing Ben out of his bed. She had heard quite enough from him for one night, thank you very much.

'Where were you two?' said Ben angrily, as James closed the balcony doors.

'Never you mind!' replied Mary, getting into bed and pulling the blankets up over herself.

'Listen,' muttered Ben, 'there's somebody in the house.'

Mary laughed dismissively. 'That would be Wilmore, silly.'

'I'm serious,' said Ben, raising his voice. 'I heard a loud noise.'

James, who was still shutting the balcony doors, eventually said, 'You're sure you weren't dreaming?'

Ben nodded, his eyes fearful. 'Positive.'

All of a sudden, there was a series of loud echoing thuds, each a different severity and sound.

Ben turned. 'See!'

'I'll check,' said James, pulling on his robe, trying his best to remain calm.

'I'll go with you,' said Ben in a low voice.

'No, stay with Mary,' James called out as he swept out the door. Without hesitation, he ran as fast as he could down three flights of stairs, but slowed slightly when he arrived at the very last staircase. The scene before his eyes was hard to explain.

Ahead, the front door was lying open and the wind gusting through was the coldest he had ever felt. With a shiver, he hurried down the remaining stairs, across the vestibule and, using all his might, swung the thick door shut.

As he bolted the door, however, something stirred behind him. Sensing a presence, he turned.

A tall dark figure was lurking by the stairs.

Trembling, James took a few paces forward, trying to see who or what it was, but before he could walk any further, the figure by the stairs moved menacingly forward.

The light of the moon slowly revealed the strange intruder. The first thing James saw was a sword dripping with blood.

The second thing he saw brought his entire world tumbling down around him.

CHAPTER TWENTY-THREE

Truth

It took James several seconds to realise that the figure at the bottom of the staircase was his grandfather, Wilmore Clyde.

James attempted to speak, but his throat seemed to have tightened, as if a ghostly hand was squeezing hard. Arms outstretched, he ran to his grandfather. 'What happened?'

Wilmore, clutching his side, collapsed against James and, a moment later, slid down to the floor.

James peered down at his hands caked in blood. 'You're bleeding!'

'James, listen.' Wilmore shook his head. 'I'm dying. I don't have much time to explain.'

Nursing his grandfather's head on his lap, James shrieked, 'What? No, I've got to call an ambulance.' He went to leave.

'No, James, no,' cried Wilmore. 'Please hear me out. You're in grave danger. For some time now they've been searching for you.' He pulled James towards him. 'I had to meet Gilbert. I had to kill him, but I failed. He's coming here – forgive me, please.'

'What are you talking about?' cried James, trying to grasp the situation.

'James, I believe your mother is still alive. In fact, I'm sure of it.'

'My mother?' said James. 'You told me she died.'

'Listen to me, James.' Wilmore groaned. 'We don't have much time. They'll be here at any moment.'

'Who are *they*?' pressed James, wondering if he even wanted to know.

'You're not from this world, James,' cried Wilmore.

'Huh?'

Taking faint breaths, Wilmore muttered, 'You were born in Orchestra and you must return there. Only you can save your people.'

'I don't understand.'

'You are the saviour, James,' said Wilmore loudly, now mustering every bit of strength left in his frail body. 'You're heir to the throne and you must survive to defeat her – otherwise nobody will.'

James looked at his grandfather and tried to digest what he had heard. He still found it hard to believe.

'Don't let them get this,' said Wilmore. A diamond was now in his hand.

James felt like he had just witnessed a mythical creature surface from the inky depths of a lake.

The jewel before him should've been a figment of his imagination, but it wasn't. He knew that it was a diamond of Orchestra.

It was slightly larger than an egg and its colour seemed to change from light green to dark green, depending on the angle he viewed it. Whatever doubts he had about the authenticity of the story were now gone. 'It's beautiful.'

'You know what this is, don't you?' said Wilmore, holding the diamond outward, encouraging James to take it.

James nodded and eased his hand on to it. The diamond's texture was smooth; it didn't feel thousands of years old. 'I *believe* you.'

Wilmore relinquished his feeble grip. 'Then use it, my child – and wisely. Get yourself, Ben and Mary far away from here.'

'But how?'

'The diamond will grant you one wish, but you must believe in its power.'

James looked down at the diamond cradled in his hands. 'And then what will I do with it?'

'You must return it to Orchestra,' responded Wilmore.

'How?'

Wilmore smiled. 'I think you already know the answer to that. The treasure chest has been calling out to you for years. It is time. Orchestra is ready for your return.'

James paused, as if to reflect on the enormity of the information he had just been given.

Wilmore pointed to the staircase. 'The key is beneath the seventeenth stair. It lifts up and in there you will find the key to your kingdom.'

James soaked up his grandfather's words as best he could. *The key is beneath the seventeenth stair.*

Suddenly, there was a loud bang on the door; James jumped and Wilmore closed his eyes and said, with one finger pointing up the stairs, 'They're here. You have to go!'

Refusing to leave, James merely pulled his grandfather closer.

Wilmore frowned at him. 'Please do as I say.'

'I'm going nowhere!' said James, trying to lift his grandfather. 'I won't leave you here like this. I have to get help.'

The incessant banging on the door suddenly became stronger, and James could hear the splintering of wood as the door began to show signs of breakage.

Wilmore pulled James closer. 'Listen to me,' he said in a groaning voice. 'I've lived my life. I've done my job. I have shown you the path to Orchestra, just like I promised your mother I would.'

'Granddad,' said James in a voice choked with sadness, 'I can't just leave you here to die.'

'You must, James, and you know you must. I will die the death every knight of Zara dreams about. I will die protecting James Clyde.' Wilmore managed a smile. 'I wouldn't want it any other way!' Then his eyes closed.

'Granddad!'

Holding his grandfather's lifeless body in his arms, James began to sob. Then, standing up, his eyes wild with rage, he glared at the door.

CHAPTER TWENTY-FOUR

James's Task

Although tears were blinding James's vision, the surrounding sounds told him everything.

The door vibrated as the force increased from the other side, but the sturdy oak stood firm, as though it knew the importance of resisting. Wiping his eyes, he looked at the doorway.

If he had followed his heart, he would've lifted the sword from the floor, ran outside and slaughtered the person responsible for the death of his grandfather.

But he was just a boy.

If only he was 10 years older; maybe then he could've sought immediate retribution.

And yet, he had been given a task: make a wish, leave the house and return to Orchestra. He would follow his grandfather's instructions to the letter. It was like a verbal agreement; he had to honour it. Moreover, he had the diamond and a little bit of clear thinking was required.

He turned, looking up at the many lofty staircases above his head. The situation was critical. The door, he knew, would not withstand much more force and there were now obvious signs of breakage: holes had appeared around the rim, allowing moonlight through.

Everything his grandfather had told him surfaced in his mind. Using the power of the diamond, he had to get everyone out of the house. Before that, however, he had to find the key to the treasure chest underneath the seventeenth stair.

Tightening his red rope tie, he started to climb the stairs, counting aloud as he went. Then, arriving at the seventeenth stair, he dropped to his knees.

★

Outside, standing with his hands on his hips, was the man in black. 'Hit it again,' he commanded, nodding at the door.

Obeying, the Dakotas rammed the thick tree trunk into the door, shattering particles of wood.

Then they went again.

And again…

Gilbert took a few paces back, remaining silent and watching as the fearsome creatures continued their assault on the house. He looked longingly at the majestic mansion. He was very close now.

Close to the end.

Close to his glory.

Shutting his eyes, he tried to imagine a time when all this would be over. How he longed for that moment! How he longed for a life of peace and comfort! As a man of advancing years, he knew his time had to come soon. He opened his eyes and smiled, feeling optimistic. *Tonight,* he thought. *Tonight!*

★

Having located the key and placed it in his pocket, James now knelt at the head of the second staircase, waiting for whoever was outside to break the door down.

At that moment, the door shattered and James felt his pulse racing. He would soon have an answer to just one of the many questions that troubled his mind. Perhaps the most important one: *who* had killed his grandfather?

- CHAPTER TWENTY-FIVE -

A Vital Few Words

When he saw the man in black, James was overcome with rage. He memorised the man's features – the moustache, the cold dark eyes and the thinning hair. He knew to remember the black clothing and the evil stare. Revenge would be sought. *Not yet, but one day!*

At that moment came a roar so loud and terrifying that James almost dropped the diamond. Looking again at the vestibule, his eye was drawn to two more figures standing either side of the man in black.

Two figures he knew were not human. Red lights beamed around the house, coming dangerously close to his position.

James swallowed hard as five more dark forms entered the house, each one armed with a sword. *Time to go,* he thought, getting to his feet and slipping the diamond into the pocket of his robe.

Quickly, he ran up the remaining stairs and, gripping the banister, began his ascent of the next one.

It was then that James heard the man in black speak for the very first time. The voice wasn't loud and he missed most of the sentence as he was running so frantically.

He did, however, catch a vital few words: "The diamond", "James Clyde" and "Kill".

CHAPTER TWENTY-SIX

Leap of Faith

Stumbling with exhaustion, James shouldered the door of his room open and fell inside. 'We have to get out of here right now!' Getting to his feet, he looked around.

Nothing.

The beds were empty, as was the room. 'Where are you?' he shouted, worried now. He walked forward, listening for a sound other than his own footsteps.

Heavy sobbing suddenly broke the silence and he saw that the balcony doors were slightly ajar. He ran quickly outside where he found Ben and Mary sprawled out on the floor, crying and shaking.

He moved towards them, aware they had witnessed everything. 'Look,' he said, lowering down and placing a consoling arm around them, 'we have to get out of here.'

After a moment, Ben and Mary wiped their eyes, climbed gingerly to their feet and linked hands with James.

'*Where* will we go?' sobbed Mary, clutching her doll. 'We're trapped.'

'We're done for!' added Ben.

'No, we're not,' said James, lifting the diamond from his pocket. He looked out at the land and an idea popped into his head. Quickly, he placed his right hand over the diamond in his left and, enunciating his words, he said, 'I wish to be able to fly.'

At once, his hands began to glow and jets of green light radiated through the gaps in between his fingers. He looked on in wonderment as the lights filled every corner of the room.

When the lights had eventually faded, the children looked at one another in sheer disbelief.

Shocked, James peered down at the glittering diamond in his hand and, although he felt no different, he decided to place his trust in the diamond and the word of his grandfather.

'Well,' said Mary, 'did it work?'

'I can't be sure,' said James, his eyes lingering on the diamond.

The consternation on Ben's face was quite evident. 'What d'you mean you can't be sure?' he cried. 'It either worked or it didn't!'

James pocketed the diamond, then nodded at the sky. 'There's only one way to find out.'

'I hate it when he says that,' said Ben.

Mary glanced at James, wondering if he'd gone mad.

'Listen,' said James, raising his voice, 'whoever is downstairs has come here to kill us. They've already killed my grandfather. We've no other choice.' He extended a hand to Ben, who, although reluctant, finally grabbed it.

James nodded. 'Good! Now, Mary, you're next – please take my hand.'

Mary seemed to consider it for a moment before finally grasping James's other hand. 'Okay, so what now?'

James smiled, his expression one of wild anticipation. 'We're going for a little spin.'

★

Three storeys below, the Dakotas roared and followed Gilbert's outstretched fingers.

Some scattered on foot around the first storey of the house, while others flew upwards and searched the other floors.

Gilbert's eyes followed the creatures up the staircases. He was starting to wonder if he would ever get his hands on the last diamond.

Tonight, he feared it might elude him yet again. That was unthinkable; but he knew that the Dakotas had a better chance of finding James Clyde and the diamond than he ever would.

He knew this because Dakotas were relentless creatures. They never tired, never stopped, nor did they ever feel pity or remorse. Whether it was a young child or an old woman, the Dakotas would kill regardless. Gilbert was their master and they obeyed his commands. He had, however, no bond with the creatures.

That would be impossible.

The Dakotas had no feelings; no moral conscience; no ability to feel sympathy. Their instinct was to kill and therefore death followed them around like a shadow.

So when their master, Gilbert, ordered them to kill James Clyde, the Dakotas didn't have to think twice about it; there was no debate or discussion on the matter – James Clyde would simply have to die.

★

The children stood on the balcony, breathing in the cold air as they contemplated jumping. Mary was now having second thoughts and had freed her hand from James's grasp.

'Mary, please,' said James, looking down at her, 'I need you to take my hand.'

'Let's just hide,' said Mary, already buttoning up her pink nightdress in preparation for the cold December night.

'Mary,' Ben yelled, 'they're in the house. For goodness' sake, give James your hand!'

'Okay, alright,' said Mary, offering her small hand.

James held Mary's hand softly, as a father might a frightened daughter. 'Don't be afraid,' he said. 'Trust me.'

Clasping her doll, Mary smiled; she always trusted him.

Meanwhile, four rooms away, a Dakota detected sound. Its huge eyes scanned back and forth, searching relentlessly for its prey. It let out a beckoning roar and two more Dakotas followed down the long corridor. Then, drawing their swords, they moved ever closer…

★

The children were now standing on the railing of the balcony, a gust of wind away from falling. There was a mixture of excitement and fear running through James's body.

He looked down at the ground.

This was it.

There were only two ways this would end: they would either jump to their deaths or the diamond would enable him to fly. He was gambling with their lives. Even if it was a magical diamond, would it work after so many years?

One way or the other, he knew he would soon have his answer. He glanced at Ben, who was holding his left hand, then at Mary, who was holding his right. 'Don't let go of my hands!' he said loudly.

Ben gave a nervous smile. He had no intention of letting go.

Together they lifted their arms into the air, like acrobats preparing for a death-defying jump.

'Here goes,' said James, glancing at Ben, then Mary, then back at Ben. 'Are you both ready?'

Ben and Mary gave unconvincing nods.

James remained focused. 'I'll jump first,' he said, speaking very clearly now. 'No matter what happens, we keep our hands together at *all* times.'

Ben gazed downwards, his worried eyes drawn to the slabs of stone far below. 'Wait, James,' he said quietly. 'Maybe Mary's right. Perhaps we should hide!'

Mary looked up at him disappointedly.

'It's too late for that.' James looked at the sky once more and sucked in the cold air. Then he paused, trying to imagine himself flying; trying to visualise the sensation of the wind hitting his face.

He could just about do it, but it was still a leap of faith. The risk involved was huge. He squeezed Ben and Mary's hands, just to make sure he still had them clutched in his. Peering down, his mind went blank, devoid of any negative thoughts.

Then, taking a deep breath, he jumped.

CHAPTER TWENTY-SEVEN

The Pursuit

As the stony ground, layered with snow, came closer, James's mind suddenly began working again. Thoughts came back, none of them positive. *What was I thinking? I've killed us all! I should've jumped alone; found out for myself.*

'You can…' Ben managed, before his words became inaudible in the whistling wind.

You can what? James thought, plummeting.

What had Ben said? *You can just go and jump from a window yourself the next time? You can at least apologise for throwing us out of a window?*

James knew Ben would never say any of those things. Ben would encourage him, tell him he could do it. *I can do it!*

That's it!

You can do it!

I can do it!

And he could.

By sheer force of will, James soared upwards and into the air, flying through the sky with the grace of a sparrow in the height of summer.

The night was exceptionally cold, but he didn't mind: it heightened his sense of power. He felt *free,* as if he had been released from invisible shackles. Cutting through the sky, he glanced across at Ben, expecting a word of congratulations, but he didn't get it.

Instead, Ben said, 'We've got company.'

James glanced over his shoulder. *Why am I not surprised?*

Dakotas were streaming out of numerous windows and tailing closely behind, their unblinking red eyes locked on the children.

Turning again, James upped the speed of his flight. He changed direction a few times, trying to lose his pursuers, but the creatures just kept pace effortlessly, moving ever closer. 'Hold on, Mary,' he cried, 'I'm going to try and go faster.'

Mary, clutching her doll under one arm, gripped James's hand and braced herself.

James – a lot more comfortable flying now – moved at his maximum speed through the air, shocked by how natural his movements were.

His instincts were that of a bird, born to command the sky. He had no idea how he could fly so naturally, but it was pointless trying to fathom it. It would be like trying to understand how he could walk or run. He could fly and, as far as he was concerned, that's all he needed to know.

'C'mon, hurry up, they're gaining on us,' shouted Ben, waving his own free hand in a bid to increase their speed.

James grimaced. 'I'm going as fast as I can,' he shouted back through the whistling wind, guessing that the Dakotas had years of flying experience over him.

'Look!' cried Mary, pointing downwards, 'we can lose them in that forest.'

James looked closer at the forest far below. It did look promising. All the treetops were shaped like broccoli and the foliage would surely hide them. Decreasing his velocity, his determined eyes pinpointed the darkest part of the forest.

A moment later, the dragon-like creatures dipped one wing and lifted the other, following the children downwards into the vast expanse of trees.

When the children lowered into the forest, they found a thick tree with an even thicker branch and curled up tightly, certain that they would be safe.

And yet, as he held Mary close, James reminded himself that their safety was a mere illusion, ready to be shattered at any moment.

CHAPTER TWENTY-EIGHT

The Forest

James grimaced as he watched the creatures move intently from tree to tree, their swords slashing into the thick foliage. Soon the faint outline of a creature stood far below.

Suddenly, it emitted a high-pitched roar. In an instant, what looked like five more Dakotas came forward, then another two, all looking up at the tree, lit dimly by the moonlight.

Peering down, James knew they were in deep trouble. Indeed, he thought it would take a miracle for them to escape from this. Looking to his right, he spotted an owl resting on a nearby branch.

Encumbered by leaves, he managed to kick the branch upon which the owl was perched and the bird hooted and fluttered into the night sky.

The Dakotas, reacting on instinct, chased the owl.

Shaking, the children watched as the red lights gradually vanished from sight.

James exhaled. It felt as though it was the first decent breath he had taken in minutes.

'Are they gone?' whispered Mary, her eyes darting around the sky.

James nodded.

'Phew!' said Ben. 'That was close, wasn't it?'

James held out his hands. 'Right, let's go!'

Moments later, he flew aimlessly, his mind reverting back to the tragic events of the night. He took solace in the fact that his grandfather's last wish had been granted.

'I think we're safe now,' said Ben.

James suddenly noticed Mary had barely said a word since they had left the forest. 'Mary, are you alright?'

'Yeah,' said Mary, peering downwards, 'this is so cool!'

James felt a wondrous sense of excitement when he looked down and saw the snowy fields beneath him. Mary was right – this was cool. He was flying! And it all came rather easily. He felt weightless, as light as a feather. Although he had been airborne for some time, he hadn't really appreciated it.

Until now.

He lowered his head, gliding this way and that, like an untethered kite caught in the breeze. The snow which had been threatening to fall from the sky for some time now finally arrived, with thick flakes floating down unremittingly.

The children could feel the snow falling on to the back of their necks, triggering involuntary shivers as they continued to fly over rooftops that were glazed with frost and snow.

Far below, the world seemed quiet.

The land was suffused with moonlight and the glory of the world was all around them – they didn't have to share it with anyone. The deserted streets and snow-blanketed fields belonged to them and them alone.

Glancing down, James could see Christmas trees flickering inside house windows. His spirits lifted. Even in this troubled hour, the dazzling lights gave him a sense of hope; a belief that everything would be alright.

As he glided over fields, he suddenly became aware of his legs dangling in the air – it was a strange sensation. He felt as though he would forget how to fly at any moment and plummet to the earth.

But he never did.

He soon realised he had nothing to fear.

He was starting to believe.

He swooped down like an eagle and glided over a lake, his body a matter of inches above the surface.

After placing Mary on his back, he trailed his fingertips along the calm surface of the water, disturbing his reflection and generating little ripples.

His eyes widened.

It was at that specific point, the moment he felt the icy water running through his fingers, that James Clyde realised he had been given something special.

From now on, his life would change dramatically – he would be able to do things that other people could only dream about. He now had a unique gift that could help people.

Some time later, he flew over a quiet town where the golden clock tower began booming for three in the morning. The hour hardly registered with him. His mind was a vacuum, empty of thought.

His eardrums ringing, he cleared the clock tower and maintained his speed over a wide bridge, which lay over a long river. He barely knew where he was going – just to continue flying seemed like a pretty good idea. Besides, he wanted to continue. He enjoyed the solitude of the sky. Up here, it was his world.

Within minutes, the town had passed like a dream and they found themselves in the countryside, where James's flight started to slow. He had wanted to find a quiet place now for some time and this forest area was perfect.

There was a large lake, much like the one he had passed earlier, and he went quickly towards it.

Carefully, he set Ben and Mary on the ground. Then he sat down on a large rock beside the lake, thankful for the rest.

He took a good hard look at his reflection in the inky water, wondering if there was more he could've done. His grandfather was dead. Their freedom and safety had come at a heavy price.

And yet, a lot of questions still lingered; why had his grandfather left it so long to tell him the truth about Orchestra and the diamond?

Finding out tonight, under such emotional circumstances, left it very hard for him to digest all the information.

He picked up a stone and threw it in the lake, listening as the water plopped. What was he supposed to do now?

Ben looked at Mary, then at James. 'What is it, James?' he said softly. 'You could've done nothing more for your granddad.'

'I'm a coward, Ben,' said James plaintively, managing words in between his sobs. 'I just let my grandfather die.'

Ben, frowning, said, 'Come off it, James, there was nothing more you could've done. And you're definitely not a coward. I mean, you saved us. Besides, we can't be sure what type of man your granddad was anymore. He led those… Those –'

'Dakotas,' said Mary.

'Exactly,' replied Ben. 'He led them to us and he knew the man who killed him. It doesn't look good, James!'

James nodded, but as far as he was concerned, his grandfather's death could and *should* have been avoided. There was a long silence and James used the time to collect his thoughts.

Although he knew that Ben and Mary had already heard some of his conversation with his grandfather, he now felt it was the right moment to reveal everything to them. 'Granddad told me Orchestra was real and that I had to return there.'

'He said that Orchestra was real?' Ben's eyebrows rose behind his large glasses. 'The same Orchestra from the stories?'

James nodded. 'Yeah.'

Ben would've burst out laughing if he didn't already know that James was serious. 'Who was that man at the house and what did he want with us?' he said crossly.

James felt like he was being interrogated. 'I honestly don't know,' he replied, looking at Ben. 'Don't you trust my granddad?'

Ben looked away.

James could feel his lower lip quivering. 'Why?'

Ben hung his head. 'I don't know who to trust anymore.'

'Well, believe me,' said James, 'we can trust Wilmore Clyde.'

Mary, listening attentively, sat quietly on a rock and took in the heated conversation. She played with her doll occasionally and moved her eyes back and forth between James and Ben.

'The answer behind all this is in that treasure chest,' said James. 'We have to go back to the house.'

Ben started to squint. 'Listen, James – your granddad brought that man to the house. Can we really trust him?'

James hesitated, then turned. 'I know we can.' Then, getting to his feet, he held out his hands. 'We're going back to the house!'

- CHAPTER TWENTY-NINE -

Treasure Chest

James's eyes began to water, obscuring his vision, but not nearly enough to miss seeing the magnificent house far below. The snow fell heavily, lashing into the children's faces.

James fought through the blizzard and swooped downwards, his robe ruffling in the wind behind him. Then, slowing down, he landed on the front garden and peered around.

Everywhere looked fine, or as fine as it possibly could under the circumstances, but he would have to be careful. He was working on the assumption that the man called Gilbert had left the house, but what if he hadn't?

James brushed these thoughts to one side. There simply wasn't time to think about anything other than the treasure chest. 'I won't be long,' he said, turning to Ben and Mary.

'No, James,' cried Mary, 'don't go in alone. Take me with you.'

James shook his head. 'I'll be back.'

Then he was gone, already flying high into the air. He glided over the car and flew upwards, to where the balcony doors were rocking in the wind.

Craning his neck, he tried to see into the room. He hovered in mid-air, thinking and listening. Then he drifted towards the railing, trying to catch a better look. The room appeared to be empty, but he was suspicious. Tonight had made him so.

Lowering on to the railing, his slippers suddenly went from

under him and his knees buckled. Falling backwards, he instinctively grabbed the railing and held on.

A moment later, feeling incredibly foolish, he let go of the railing and floated. *Old habits die hard,* he thought. Then, crossing his arms, he began to laugh.

How powerful he felt right now!

He had nothing to fear. In three thrusts of his arms and legs, he was inside his bedroom, looking around. The once safe appearance of his room had been tarnished forever.

Moving further inside, he tried to recollect everything his grandfather had told him. He had to get to Orchestra via the treasure chest.

What else? Think!

Then it suddenly came to him – he was a king; the saviour to a world beyond the one in which he lived.

It was quite a stretch, but then he reminded himself that he had used a magical diamond and just flown across the sky as easily as a bird in flight. Perhaps it was true.

From outside, a chorus of voices shouted, 'What's keeping you? We're frozen out here. We're coming up, James.'

James had almost forgotten about them. *They're coming up!* 'No!' he shouted at the top of his voice. 'Don't come up here! I'll be down in a moment.'

'Well, hurry up then,' Ben shouted angrily from the garden below.

At once, James sprinted out the door of his room and along the corridor. When he came to the first staircase, he grabbed the banister and threw himself over, powering downwards.

Even running this before would've taken quite some time, but with the ability of flight he merely had to jump over the first banister and allow himself to fall towards the bottom, his robe acting like a parachute behind him.

When he hit the bottom, his slippers pounded the floor with incredible force; it felt as though the soles of his feet were on fire.

He danced on the spot, hopping from one foot to the other. When recovered, he looked around the vestibule.

His eyes met some terrible sights: the wind gusted through the gap where the door had once stood and his grandfather lay on the floor, a dark pool of blood around him now.

James felt a lump in his throat. He had no idea why he'd flown to the front door when he knew such a terrible sight awaited him. Perhaps he needed to see his grandfather one last time, but the scene he was looking at would haunt his dreams forever.

He looked away, sickened by what he saw. Quickly, he flew to the top floor, where he opened a different window of the house.

With that done, he stretched his two hands over his head, clenched his fists closed and powered outside once more. When he landed in the garden, Ben and Mary ran towards him.

'What took you so long?' said Ben, his teeth chattering, his arms wrapped around his body.

'Sorry.'

'Are they gone?' said Mary, her frightened eyes studying the house.

James nodded, holding out his hands. 'Yeah. C'mon.'

Joining hands, James whisked them into the air and flew to the top of the house, to where the window was lying open. Floating effortlessly through, he made his way towards the mysterious doorway where they had been only hours earlier.

As the door came into sight, Ben looked incredulous. 'This is pointless, James,' he cried. 'Why the hell have you brought us here again? The treasure chest is locked.' He sighed. 'I mean, we've already tried it tonight.'

From the deep pocket of his bed robe, James removed the key his grandfather had given him. 'We have this now.'

Ben gasped. 'Is that what I think it is?'

'I hope so,' said James, taking a good look at it.

'Who gave you that?' asked Mary.

'Granddad,' James told her.

'We can't trust him, James.' It broke Ben's heart to say it, but he felt he had to be brutally honest. 'It could be a trap.'

'It's not, Ben,' said James, the tears rolling down his cheeks. 'I saw the look in his eyes, you didn't. I trust my grandfather and so should you.'

'I did trust him, James,' cried Ben, 'but I don't know if we can trust him now. That's all I'm saying.'

Sighing, James looked down at the floor in disbelief.

'I trust Wilmore,' said Mary, finally deciding to voice her opinion. 'I think we should open it.'

Reluctantly, Ben approached James and said, 'I hope you're both right.'

James, leading the way, walked towards the door in silence, while Ben and Mary held hands and followed closely behind.

Strangely, everywhere appeared dark and the mysterious lights which had become such a familiar sight were nowhere to be seen.

Inside the room, Ben flicked the light switch, but it didn't work. After taking a few more steps forward, he felt the crunching of the glass from the broken bulb under his slippers.

'Quick, Ben,' said James, 'light that candle and bring it over here.'

Ben lifted a match from beside the stand, struck it, then lit the candle and carried it towards the treasure chest.

'Do you think that Wilmore left us another diamond?' said Mary, holding her doll close.

'No idea,' James told her.

The children fell to their knees before the chest. James, whose heart was pounding, held the key in his sweaty hand and lifted it towards the lock. Inserting the key, he found to his delight that it fitted in the lock. *This is it!*

Breathing heavily, he moved the key clockwise. To his utter amazement, he heard a loud click and felt the lock loosen.

'Now lift it up!' said Ben, his eyes dilating behind his glasses.

Together, they heaved the heavy lid open and watched as it hit the ground with a thud. Gathering around, they peered inside.

They could barely believe it.

'Nothing!' Ben roared, illuminating the inside of the chest with the candle. He turned to James angrily. 'Now do you believe me? He took everything for himself. I knew we couldn't trust him.'

Mary turned away, looking disappointed.

To James, it was a lot worse than a let down; it was soul-destroying. Nothing made sense now, and for the first time, his loyalty was challenged. Drained by emotion, he dropped to his knees.

For several minutes he knelt there, staring at the treasure chest, wondering what could possibly have gone wrong. Then he suddenly felt a breeze on his face, as if somebody had opened a window.

The wind gradually increased and the candle in Ben's hand went out. 'What's going on, James?' he cried, letting the candle stand fall to the floor.

Getting to his feet, James replied, 'Your guess is as good as mine.'

'James!' cried Mary, taking his hand.

A faint flicker of light suddenly broke through the pitch blackness.

James smiled. The light was coming from the treasure chest. Holding hands and keeping very close together, the children made their way towards the light. With each step, the breeze seemed to grow stronger.

Fighting through the wind, they huddled around the treasure chest. Just then, the light vanished, followed immediately afterwards by the calming of the wind.

James, opening his eyes, sensed something was different. A hunch.

He knew this was it.

Peering down, he jumped when two green arms rose from the solid base and grabbed him by the shoulders. 'Hold on!' he cried, wrapping his hands around Ben and Mary's wrists. Hauled inside, the bottom of the chest opened like a trapdoor and they fell through.

James felt like he was falling down a dark tunnel. He could see nothing and could only hear his own heart throbbing. Then the air became very clean and clear, as if an oxygen mask had been shoved over his mouth.

Then came light. Sunlight. Dizzy, dazed, he tried to fly, but found he couldn't. Spinning through the air, he thought of Ben and Mary, aware of their absence. Then his head cracked on the ground and, with a groan, he turned on to his back.

Through partially closed eyes, James looked up at the sky. It was the bluest sky he had ever seen. He tried to fight against his flickering eyes, tried to focus on the cloudless sky, but the darkness was closing in on him.

Only a speck of blue now remained in his vision, but before his world turned black, he could smell the enveloping scent of flowers.

PART 2

CHAPTER THIRTY

Orchestra

Ben was falling.

Of that he could be quite sure.

His feet kicked madly for land, but found only endless air. Out of the corner of his eye, he saw Mary, her face as frightened as his own.

James, however, was nowhere to be seen. *Uh-oh!*

Far below, a large body of turquoise water lay. Just before impact, Ben felt his glasses slip down the bridge of his nose and watched as they zoomed past his face. 'Deep breath, Mary!' he cried before they thundered feet-first into the surface of the water, generating a giant wave.

Plummeting, he tightened his grip around Mary's hand, but suddenly, just when he thought everything would be alright, his body snapped backwards. Despite his best efforts, he could feel Mary's fingers slipping through his grasp.

Blowing air bubbles, he looked madly around, but Mary was nowhere to be seen. Quickly, he fought his way upwards, towards the surface, inhaling some much-needed air when he got there. 'Mary!' he called out, treading water. After a few moments of silence, he pinched his nose and dove under again.

Almost an hour later, and after many failed attempts to find his sister, he reluctantly swam to land and sat sadly down beside a tree. He took another look at the water, hoping for a miracle.

'MARY!'

There was no answer. Then he eyed a disturbance on the surface of the water. It was promising.

He ran forward eagerly. Before him, the water bubbled to life. Hope turned quickly to despair. Only yards away, bobbing on the water's surface was Mary's porcelain doll. He walked over and, using a long tree branch, towed the doll to land.

He wondered if Mary – who he knew couldn't swim – had somehow made it to land. Staring out into the vast water, he knew it was highly unlikely. How could this be happening? Only hours ago, he had been sleeping soundly, but now he had lost both James and Mary.

He had never felt so alone. Hanging his head, he collapsed to the ground and wept bitterly.

★

James Clyde awoke slowly, his aching body buried in a meadow of lush daffodils. The warm breeze told him it was the height of summer, but where was the snow? More importantly, though, where were Ben and Mary?

Coated in clay, he got to his feet and looked around. The sky was cloudless and the glorious sun beamed brightly. Gazing to his right, he saw a long dense forest.

Was he in Orchestra? It appeared so. And yet…

He just couldn't bring himself to believe it.

Looking around again, an idea struck him. The meadow in which he stood came to an end just yards ahead. Whatever lay beyond that point might ring a bell with him. As he walked forward, enjoying the warmth of the sun, he suddenly remembered the diamond.

Reaching into his pocket, he lifted out the sparkling jewel. Relief washed over him. It could have fallen out anywhere.

Just then, he heard the sounds of branches snapping from

inside the forest. Like a balloon in the breeze, he rose upwards, trying to see if anybody was coming.

Nothing.

Quickly, he returned to the ground and pocketed the diamond. As far as he could see, the only way out of this situation would be to fly – go elsewhere – but a part of him was hoping that perhaps Ben and Mary were coming towards him. 'Who's there?' he shouted at the top of his voice.

Nobody spoke.

Thinking he should have another look, he lifted off the ground and glanced around, but nobody else could be seen.

Without delay, he returned to the meadow, lifted a large rock and swung it from side to side. 'Show yourself!'

A soft voice spoke. 'Please put the rock down.'

James had no intention of putting the rock down until he saw who he was dealing with. 'Who's there? Who said that?'

'I did,' responded the voice. 'Down here.'

James felt a slight tug on his robe and, looking down, eyed a very small man, the likes of which he'd never seen before.

The man was dressed entirely in green, apart from a pointed red hat that sat elegantly on his short blond hair.

James stared at him for several seconds. Then, unable to come up with a rational explanation, he asked, 'Who are you?'

'My name is Grampian.' He lifted the hat from his head and bowed. 'I am an orchin.'

'A what?'

'An orchin,' repeated Grampian. 'I am the leader of the orchins of Orchestra.'

James, deciding it was best not to question any of this, simply nodded his head.

Grampian said, 'Do you know where you are, James?'

James looked around, admiring his surroundings yet again. 'Am I in Orchestra?'

Grampian gave a nod. 'Zara, to be precise. The land of your birth.'

'I was born here?'

Grampian smiled and began to walk towards the end of the meadow.

James followed closely behind.

'You've a great deal to learn,' said Grampian, 'and we will help you in whatever way we can.'

With the end of the meadow now in sight, James stopped suddenly and extended a hand, stopping Grampian from going any further. 'How do I get home?'

'Well, you need a transporter for that,' Grampian told him, 'but we were all hoping you would stay for quite some time.'

'We?'

Grampian pointed to the left. 'Take another look at the Zaran forest.'

Suddenly, James could see branches stirring. Within seconds, hundreds of orchins had appeared, all of them smiling and pointing at him. He looked back at Grampian, who continued pushing through the daffodils.

James knew he was standing very high up. Other than that, however, he had no idea what could possibly be waiting for him at the end of the meadow. As he neared the edge, his curiosity was soon satisfied.

Grampian waved a tiny hand forward. 'Welcome home.'

James stopped and let his eyes rove around Orchestra. He had never seen such a place. Finally, he managed a word. *'Outstanding.'* Directly opposite him was a large mountain, much like the one he was standing on, covered with an abundance of red roses. On his left was another, this one with a giant cascading waterfall thundering powerfully into a body of water below. Peering down, he saw the foam of the waves crashing against the rocks. He could feel the spray of the water on his cheeks.

'The Orchestra Ocean,' Grampian pointed out. '23 miles long, I'll have you know.'

James gave his arm a tight squeeze, but to his utter amazement, instead of waking up in his bed, he still found himself looking at the most breathtaking sight his eyes had ever fallen upon.

Grampian edged closer. 'No dream, James,' he said. 'In fact, I'd say you've never been more awake in your entire life.'

There was a momentary silence, as if to fully appreciate the beauty of the land.

'Would you believe, James,' Grampian went on, 'that you are the owner of every flower, every blade of grass and every drop of water that you are looking at?'

James let the thought linger. *I own everything?* Turning around, he stared at Grampian in sheer disbelief. 'How can that be?'

'Come with me and you'll find out,' said Grampian.

James hesitated.

'Don't be afraid,' said Grampian. 'You're safe now.'

Uncertain, James followed Grampian back through the meadow and into the Zaran forest, where they set off on the long trek, accompanied by the rest of the orchins.

★

Meanwhile, Ben had wandered far from his original position. He had just walked up a precipitous bank and now lay face down on the stony ground.

What he had just achieved was no small feat, considering the bank was steep and overgrown, but more than that, he had conquered it all wearing a pair of leather slippers.

With frozen fingers, he wiped dirt from his lips and looked up. His surroundings were dark and miserable, but his eye was drawn to one particular tree, standing all alone to his right. Scrawled in red paint on its trunk were a series of words. He read the words through chattering teeth – *THE FOREST OF THE DEAD*.

CHAPTER THIRTY-ONE

The Forest of the Dead

Although tempted to leave at first, Ben now found himself walking slowly forward. On either side of him were two large and shadowy forests, separated by a meandering lane that stretched out as far as the eye could see.

Looking at the forest to his left, he saw something that baffled him. Strangely, some trees had been chopped down. In their place were giant holes the size of craters.

Odd, he thought, moving further forward. His mind was still on the gaping holes when he glimpsed a sudden rustling of the leaves in the forest to his right.

He stopped, not sure whether he should proceed as planned. Keeping his gaze on the trees, he thought he could see large shadows, all of them moving around the forest in a very busy manner.

Fear set in. *I shouldn't be here!* He had hoped that Mary might've strayed up here, but looking back now, he could tell that a little girl like her would never have been able to climb such a steep bank.

A sharp voice spoke, and he turned once again to the forest. The shadows had stopped moving, as if they had suddenly become aware of his presence.

That can't be good! Turning, he jogged back towards the bank.

All of a sudden, from within the forest, twigs began to crunch and the sound of running feet could be heard.

Ben's jog developed into a desperate sprint. Not until he heard a loud humming sound behind him did he realise his life was in danger.

A last burst of energy saw him to the bank and adrenaline carried him over. Down and down he ran, glancing over his shoulder as he went. Stumbling on a protruding rock, he fell over and tumbled all the way to the bottom.

After a moment to recover, he peered upwards.

Nobody was there. Had he imagined it?

Overhead, the birds chirped and the grey clouds had cleared. It was perhaps late afternoon and uncomfortably hot.

Exhausted, he crawled under the nearest tree. Then, curling up, he drifted into a deep sleep.

★

In the Zaran forest, James Clyde continued his seemingly endless journey. His feet were sore, the harsh terrain finally beginning to take its toll on his well-worn slippers.

Something suddenly struck him. 'Hold on!' he blurted, seizing Grampian's arm. 'I came here with two other people – a boy and a girl.'

'They're safe,' said Grampian with a nod. 'I give you my word.'

James had got Grampian's word. That should've made him feel better, but it didn't. Ben and Mary weren't with him; that was all that mattered.

'We're almost there,' said Grampian with pride.

'Almost where?' asked James, looking around.

Grampian smiled. 'You'll see.'

One mile later, after walking in a straight line for some time, Grampian turned to James, pointed a finger forward and said, 'Just through those trees.'

James's eyes were already on the trees. Pushing through, he found himself in a part of the forest that looked very different to every other. There were no trees and his slippers now stood on white marble stone.

Up ahead, sitting in the middle of the courtyard, was a wishing well made of stone. He turned around, surprised. 'Where are we?'

'We are *here*,' said Grampian.

James smiled. *I'm glad we cleared that up.* He turned his attention back to the courtyard. What was he doing here?

'Just make your way towards the well,' said Grampian, pointing.

James obeyed, knowing that he would get answers quicker if he did so.

Grampian followed. Side by side, they walked forward until they came to within yards of the wishing well.

'Stop,' said Grampian, nodding to the ground. 'Stay right there.'

James looked down and saw a black circle around his feet. 'What now?'

'James Clyde,' said Grampian, 'please kneel.'

★

Ben awoke to the sound of laughter, which he had heard many times before, but never had it sounded so joyful to his ear.

It was Mary.

It's impossible, Ben thought, getting to his feet. He looked out into the water and saw Mary stranded. He had never felt such a mix of emotions.

On the one hand, he was relieved to see her, but on the other, he knew she was drowning. Panic set in. In the water, 10 feet away from Mary, a fin emerged, heading straight towards her.

'*Shark!*' Unconcerned for his own safety, Ben sprinted towards the ocean, plunged head first into the water and started swimming as fast as he could, but he knew he wasn't going to get to her in time.

The shark was about to attack. With a giant splash of the water, Mary was hoisted aloft. Then, most distressingly, she vanished under the clear water, leaving nothing but bubbles on the surface.

Floating aimlessly, Ben knew he was next. He would be swallowed up at any moment. The pain would be excruciating, but hopefully brief.

Next moment, he felt the shark whisk him up on to its back, while at the same time Mary reappeared, looking fit and healthy, which Ben thought very strange after a confrontation with a shark.

'What's wrong with you?' said Mary, noting her brother's pale complexion.

'Wait a minute!' cried Ben, daring to look down at the water, his face showing a hint of colour again. 'These aren't sharks – they're dolphins!'

Mary chuckled. 'Well, of course they're dolphins!'

Dolphins, propelled by their flippers, moved through the ocean, each one of them differently coloured.

Minutes later, the dolphins dropped the children off safely at the bank. As Ben and Mary wrung their pyjamas dry, they finally had a chance to talk.

'What happened to you?' said Ben. 'I was worried sick.'

Mary didn't know where to begin. 'Well, for a start,' she said, 'just after we got separated, I almost drowned, but thankfully the dolphins saved me and since then, they've taken me all over the ocean.'

'I thought I'd lost you, blondie,' said Ben, his eyes moist.

Mary ran forward to give Ben a hug. 'You boys can be so silly sometimes. I'm eight years old and quite capable of looking after myself.'

'But you can't swim,' sobbed Ben. 'What else was I supposed to think?'

'C'mon, let's find James,' said Mary, taking Ben's hand and walking into the forest.

CHAPTER THIRTY-TWO

The Saviour Returns

James's eyes scanned the courtyard. Apart from the well, it was completely bare. He had no clue as to what he might be doing here. Up ahead, the Zaran forest appeared to continue. Behind him, the orchins stood quietly.

He remained positioned on one knee, as if in preparation for prayer.

Questions, however, still nagged at him. What was he doing here? Why did he have to kneel?

He looked at the well and noticed that the hanging bucket had started to sway slightly. It made a squeaking sound as it rocked back and forth.

He thought this strange – there was no wind.

Two more minutes went by.

Five.

10.

Nothing.

Then the bucket slowed and eventually halted completely.

James, breathing heavily, looked around.

Something had changed.

A blinding flash of light filled the courtyard for a moment, then dimmed.

Through the gaps of the fingers covering his eyes, James saw the silhouette of a woman standing amongst the puffy white clouds. She looked like a ghost; a spirit back from the dead. Her face was beautiful, with ageless white skin and large blue eyes that never seemed to blink. Her slender body was covered by a long white tunic that descended over the clouds.

Time to wake up, James thought. *It's a figment of my imagination. I don't believe it!*

A woman's voice spoke, soft and gentle. 'James, I am *not* your imagination. Look at me. Believe, James Clyde.'

James looked up and saw the spirit still hovering in mid-air. Slowly, he lifted his hands away from his face. 'Who are you?'

'I am a messenger.'

James smiled. 'You look like an angel.'

The figure of light smiled back and said, somewhat proudly, 'James, you've been brought here for a reason.'

James shook his head. 'I'm 11 years old. What could I – ?'

'Hear this now: one day you will be the greatest protector Orchestra has ever known.' The spirit smiled, as if to suggest she had some good news. 'I will bestow upon you a gift for your journey.'

A moment later, a golden sword descended slowly, as if by an invisible string. Lower and lower it went, until the pommel touched James's hand.

He flexed his fingers, lowered his face to the level of the sword and moved his eyes this way and that, studying the entire thick blade. He never touched it, though; he felt afraid to do so.

'This sword is divine,' said the spirit.

James reached for the sword, then hesitated.

Almost sensing his fear, the weapon lowered magically into his hands. Astonished, he looked up, his eyes fixed on the spirit.

'I know you have many questions. Seek the knights.'

Then, without warning, she pointed at James, who was immediately lifted off the ground with his newly acquired sword still clutched in both hands.

The spirit placed her hand into a cloud beside her and appeared to take a fragment of the cloud with her. Then she threw the fragment at James, whose clothes were instantly transformed from pyjamas to a dazzling white outfit.

The spirit said, 'I will protect and watch over you in your quest, James Clyde.' Then, without another word, the ghostly glow vanished from the heavens as quickly as it had first appeared.

A hush fell over the courtyard as James rose, sword in hand, and looked around. Although it felt like he had been talking to the spirit for just a couple of minutes, he now realised it must have been longer; for the day had ended, replaced by a bright night.

Grampian broke through the crowd, walked over to James and said, 'Nobody is to know what you saw.'

James narrowed his eyes. 'You mean you didn't see any of that?'

Grampian smiled. 'We are merely following centuries-old instructions,' he replied darkly.

James looked at Grampian with interest, but before he could ask anything else, a round of applause went up. He spun around, struggling to grasp the situation.

When the rapturous round of applause had eventually faded, Grampian turned to James. 'Master, you must be hungry.' He smiled. 'Let's get you something to eat.'

James raised an arm and said, 'No, please, I have to find Ben and Mary.'

Grampian gave a nod. 'You will find them at the water's ledge beside Orchestra Ocean.'

James fished into the pocket of his new costume, lifted out the diamond and showed it to Grampian. A question seemed to roll off his lips. 'What should I do with this?'

'You're the leader now, master,' replied Grampian. 'You should keep it.'

James sighed, his eyes lingering on the diamond. 'Please, Grampian. Please keep it for me until I come back.'

Grampian nodded and took the diamond. 'Of course.'

Although James wanted Grampian to have the diamond, he

still felt sad parting with it. The diamond almost seemed like a family heirloom at this stage. Still, he knew it was the right thing to do. The diamond would be a lot safer with Grampian.

'Master,' said Grampian, 'I must warn you not to travel any further than the water. Where the water stops is where the evil starts.' He pointed to the reddening sky. 'Night has fallen and you must get your rest.'

James nodded, and yet he was much too worried about Ben and Mary to care about getting a good night's sleep. He tucked his sword into the belt around his waist, only then noticing that his long white boots ran all the way up to his knees. Something still bothered him, though. 'Grampian?'

Grampian swivelled around, wearing a wide smile. 'Yes?'

'From now on, please call me James!'

Grampian nodded, smiling.

James smiled back, then turned. For the first time since he had arrived in Orchestra, he felt confident and strong, almost like a newer version of himself.

Moving with a swagger, he drew his sparkling sword and held it out before him like a torch. As he ran, he switched his attention to the darkening sky, focusing on the three moons he was about to ascend to.

Then, powering off the ground, he left dust in his wake.

CHAPTER THIRTY-THREE

Exploring Orchestra

Ben and Mary walked along the water's ledge of Orchestra Ocean. Mary kept her eyes on the water, trying to spot James. The sooner they found him, the better. Not for a moment, though, did she suspect James was in trouble; he was a survivor and he could fly. *A small advantage,* she thought, scanning the water's surface.

'James!' shouted Ben, looking everywhere.

'Let's split up,' suggested Mary, looking across at Ben, who glanced back at her with a wry smile and said, 'You're joking, right?'

★

James was no longer in the air; he was standing on the surface of Orchestra Ocean, ears listening for sounds.

Slowly, he began to run forward, looking at the forest to his right, trying to spot a flicker of movement in the moonlight. A moment later, he heard voices. He rose, arms by his side, using his hands almost as propellers as he flew quickly forward.

★

For a good while now, Ben and Mary had known they were totally lost. They were wandering around aimlessly, in more hope than confidence.

'Where are we, then?' asked Mary.

'Dunno,' said Ben.

Mary groaned. 'I'm starving.'

Ben let out a sigh. 'Seriously, Mary, even for a girl, you talk too much.'

'No I don't,' said Mary indignantly.

'Sometimes you do and it's really annoying.'

'Well, if you didn't always –'

'Shush,' cried Ben.

'Don't tell me to –'

'QUIET!' Ben pulled Mary towards him. 'Do you hear that?'

Mary could hear a low rumbling sound in the sky. 'What is that?'

Ben's face drained of colour. 'It's one of those flying things with red eyes!'

'Dakotas?'

'Whatever,' cried Ben. 'Let's get out of here before they have us for their supper.'

'Don't be stupid!' said Mary after a moment. 'They don't eat you.'

Ben took Mary's hand and broke into a run, dodging trees as he went. 'Is that supposed to make me feel better?'

Mary, shocked by Ben's overreaction, said, 'It could be James.'

'Trust me, it's not,' insisted Ben, his voice quivering with terror.

'Wait… Ben, Mary!' shouted James, chasing after them.

Ben continued on his way, hurdling over fallen tree branches, his frightened eyes looking straight ahead.

Mary freed herself from Ben's grasp, turned around and ran back to where James was standing.

Overjoyed, they held each other in a close embrace.

'Thank God you're here,' said Mary. 'Ben's really starting to get on my nerves.' She frowned. 'Do I talk too much?'

James chuckled and, holding Mary in his arms, he rose upwards. 'Not nearly enough!'

'Well, look who it is!' cried Ben, as James returned to the forest. 'Nice of you to finally join us.'

'Don't mention it,' said James.

'Where were you?' Ben shook his head. 'No, first tell me where we are. This is Orchestra, isn't it?'

Mary scoffed. 'Well, of course it's Orchestra,' she told him briskly. 'I guess Wilmore was telling the truth all along.'

'I guess he was,' said Ben with a sheepish shrug.

James looked at Ben, then Mary, then back at Ben. 'What happened to your glasses, and why are you both soaking wet?'

'My glasses are probably at the bottom of the ocean by now,' replied Ben.

'That also explains why we're drenched,' added Mary.

'And can you see okay?' asked James.

'Well, it's funny,' said Ben, looking around. 'Ever since I got here I can see perfectly.'

Mary nodded. 'And he hasn't squinted yet either!'

'Thanks for noticing that, blondie.' Ben grinned at James. 'Now, back to you – why do you look like a superhero?'

'Orchins gave me this outfit and this sword.' Only after saying it did James realise how bizarre the story must have sounded.

Mary flashed a smile. 'You saw an orchin?'

James nodded.

'Now that you mention an outfit,' said Ben, touching his pyjamas with a look of disgust, 'we could do with a change of clothes ourselves.'

Mary pulled James by the arm. 'Do these orchins have any clothes for a girl?'

'I'm sure they do,' replied James, who looked out across the silvery surface of the ocean, realising that he hadn't been able to explore Orchestra properly yet. He pointed upwards. 'Want to go exploring?'

Ben and Mary swapped excited looks and smiled.

'Then we will,' said James, taking Mary's hand in his and holding it gently. With great aplomb, he rose effortlessly off the ground, leaving the heels of his boots imprinted in the muddy ground.

Mary was smiling. Pressed against James, she felt safe and sound again. 'It's good to have you back, James,' she said softly, squeezing his hand.

With a smile, James pushed through the humid air, reflecting on the events that had happened since his arrival in Orchestra.

He felt as though he had entered a beautiful painting and was enjoying at first hand the wondrous use of colour. From this aerial vantage point, he could see for miles in every direction.

'James, I won't need that change of clothes after all,' said Ben, patting his pyjama top, 'I'm dry again.'

'He's right,' agreed Mary, touching her nightdress, 'I am, too.'

'Nothing quite like flying to dry your clothes, is there?' said James, who soared down through the clouds and took a sharp left, making his way along the ocean. He could hardly hide his delight as he moved inches above the water. Then, like a rocket, he launched himself upwards once more.

'Look down there,' cried Mary. James followed the direction of her outstretched finger and saw, jumping from the water below, a pod of dolphins racing each other up the ocean.

James smiled in amazement. 'They're all different colours.'

The dolphins were jumping in and out of the water, clearly putting on a show as they followed the children along the Orchestra Ocean.

James laughed. They were all back together again. Everything was as it should be.

Bowing his head, flying at an altitude more accustomed to an aircraft, he upped the speed of his flight and thundered through the sky, the wind whistling past his ears.

Up here, he felt invincible. Up here, he feared nobody. He swayed this way and that, ruling the sky with supreme authority.

Then, lowering his head, he went faster still.

- CHAPTER THIRTY-FOUR -

The Gates to Hell

As the seconds turned into minutes and the minutes turned into hours, James felt the joyful feeling in his stomach gradually change to one of dread.

Why this was happening, he couldn't say – the signs were still good. The air was warm, the night pleasant, and the luminescent moonlight shooting across the landscape only enhanced its beauty. Yet something didn't seem right.

Feeling the wind on his face, he looked around. At first glance, nothing seemed different, but he couldn't help noticing just how quiet the land had become.

The birds no longer chirped and the water was still and calm – there was complete silence.

'Look, James,' cried Mary, pointing a finger forward, 'the ocean's coming to an end.'

James slowed his flight. The water had stopped at a huge mountain that towered upwards and out of sight into the sky. 'I thought it would never end.' Swaying gently in the breeze, he gazed around. 'How far do you reckon we've flown?'

'10, maybe 15 miles,' Ben guessed.

'We'd better turn back,' said James. 'Grampian will be getting worried.'

'Who's Grampian?' asked Mary, intrigued to finally hear a name other than James and Ben.

'Oh,' said James, 'he's the leader of the orchins.'

Mary smiled. 'Are these orchins the same ones from the stories?' she asked inquisitively.

James nodded. 'Pretty much.'

'What height are they?' said Mary.

'About your height, actually,' James told her, fighting back a smile.

Ben laughed. 'That small, huh?'

'Where are the dolphins going?' said Mary, pointing down at the ocean.

James's gaze lowered to the Orchestra Ocean and he saw the dolphins fleeing as fast as their flippers could take them, back in the opposite direction.

Turning sharply around, he switched his attention back to the steep mountain before him. If Grampian was right and he did own everything, then surely he had a right to know what lay beyond this mountain?

Considering he had travelled this length, he might as well continue on a little bit further. His mind was made up.

'Let's see what's over the mountain,' he said, zooming upwards, only stopping when he was close to the mountain's summit. Drifting about seven feet from the top, he eyed a smooth crater that protruded from the mountain. This would be an ideal place for them to rest briefly.

Minutes later, feeling fully revived, he placed his hands on top of the mountain and, very carefully, brought his blue eyes over the ledge.

He took everything in: two dark forests, a long lane and black clouds overhead. The air he was breathing was noticeably cooler and a blanket of mist hung around the trees. It didn't take him long to draw the conclusion that this was Darken.

Apprehension gave way to intrigue. He returned to Ben and Mary and lifted them high into the air.

Ben frowned. 'Not this place again.'

James nudged him and said, 'Let's travel up a bit.'

Mary, shivering, said, 'Let's not.'

'Jimbo, are you serious?' said Ben. 'I've already been here once and that was more than enough.' He shook his head. 'I mean – just look at it.'

'You were here?' said James, thinking he'd heard wrong.

Ben gave a quick nod. 'I came up here looking for Mary and, let's just say, it's not a very nice place.'

'I just want to travel up a little bit,' said James, trying to find a compromise.

'Do we have a choice?' said Ben with a frown.

James began to fly. 'Nope, but I would like your support.'

'Just a little bit then,' agreed Mary finally.

A while later, after travelling at a steady pace, Ben said through chattering teeth, 'Let's turn back, James.'

James shook his head. 'Just another bit more,' he said. *Just another little bit.*

Two minutes later, as they headed into dense fog, Mary cleared her throat.

James smiled, knowing a hint when he heard one. 'Right, we'll head back.'

'Watch out!' yelled Ben, and James stopped in his tracks. To his amazement, only inches from his nose was a long black iron bar. His eyes followed the bar upwards until the mist took it from his sight. He looked left and right, where many more bars were obstructing his passage.

As he descended to the gravel, Mary said, 'What are they?'

'They're gates, aren't they?' said Ben with a deep frown.

James nodded. From a standing position, the bars looked even more menacing and foreboding, like gates to a cemetery. He squeezed his arm in between two bars, watching as it vanished in the mist.

Mary shook her head. 'Gates to where?'

'To hell, probably,' said Ben, taking a step forward and

wrapping his fingers around a bar. 'What do you reckon is in there?'

James pushed his cheeks against the bars, but the mist was so great that nothing beyond could be seen. As he kept his eyes fixed on the gates, wondering what secrets might lie beyond, he felt something brush against his leg.

Looking down, he saw a black cat rubbing up against his boots. The cat miaowed when he lifted her off the foliage.

'Where did that thing come from?' whispered Ben, looking around. 'Listen, James,' he went on, 'that's the first bit of life I've seen in this forest. We're obviously not in a very nice part of Orchestra. We shouldn't be here and you know it.'

James looked uncomfortable. 'You're right,' he said after a moment, placing the cat on to the gravel. 'Let's get out of here!' Before he could make a move, however, he heard the sound of hooves thundering along the ground.

The children glanced at one another, and Mary whispered, 'Somebody's coming!'

James paused, looking uncertain.

'We can't be seen, James,' said Ben. 'We have to hide.'

James wanted to leave, but something told him Ben was right. Reluctantly, they flew into the forest and ducked behind a gathering of trees.

Keeping as low as he could, James raised his hands, parted some branches and peered out at a large horse-drawn carriage moving like an express train along the lane.

The carriage was black, except for a few strips of gold around the rim of the door, and covering the windows on either side were embroidered purple curtains, making it look like the transport of royalty.

The driver heaved the reins of the two black stallions towards him and the wheels of the carriage came to a sudden and strident halt, leaving a trail in the gravel. As the driver jumped from the carriage, he grunted and growled fiercely, his eyes scanning everything.

He was a large man, his frame wider than a door and his torso more muscular than a heavyweight boxer. He had long hair, black eyes and an enormous nose. His tight, threadbare trousers were cut off above the knees and his giant hairy arms, which were disproportionate to the rest of his body, hung all the way to the ground.

The man stood looking at the gates. 'Open the gates!' he shouted.

Nothing happened.

'Why do they never see us coming?' he said, talking to himself now. 'She won't be happy about this.'

Listening from the forest, James was immediately struck by the tone of the man's voice. The man looked hideous; there was no question about that, but his voice sounded normal – pleasant, almost.

With a shake of his head, the man walked towards the carriage door, but then stopped suddenly to take a curious look at the forest.

Without so much as a word, the children let the branches fall back into place, lowered down on to the foliage and kept deadly still.

The horses' hooves were clopping along the ground, but other than that, James couldn't hear another sound. Had the man seen them? It seemed impossible, given the amount of trees in the forest.

Moments later, growing tired of hiding, James got to his feet and saw the large man standing beside the carriage, his eyes glaring at every leaf that so much as swayed in the breeze.

At last, the man turned. When he reached the carriage door, he heaved it open with one hand.

Watching on, the children held their breaths.

CHAPTER THIRTY-FIVE

Queen Abigail of Darken

A slim woman with raven black hair in a neat bob stepped confidently from the carriage.

James's eyes widened with interest. She was the most beautiful woman he had ever seen in his entire life. He knew this was Queen Abigail – the ruler of Darken; the woman who wanted him dead and who would stop at nothing to find him.

On her head was a gold crown, decorated by multi-coloured jewels. She had large, feline-like eyes. She wore the finest black fabric under a dark purple robe that acted like a blanket around her body.

'Your Majesty,' the man said, lowering his head reverentially.

'Why the delay?' said the queen, fiercely.

The Volen dropped to his knees, grovelling at the hem of the queen's robe. 'Forgive me, please. I wouldn't normally be so slow, but I thought I smelt an orchin.'

'In Darken?'

'Yes, Your Majesty.'

'Of all the stupid things I've heard.'

Sensing her annoyance, the Volen quickly reached into his pocket, produced a black whistle and blew into it. The instrument emitted a loud ring.

At once, lights began to appear. Through the fog, the children could see what looked like an enormous castle with numerous high towers and wide turrets.

At that moment, two more Volens stepped forward and parted the gates, allowing the queen to walk through.

Mary tapped James on the arm. 'Look at the sky,' she whispered, pointing.

Raising his eyes, James saw a familiar sight. 'Dakotas,' he said under his breath. 'I hate those things!'

'There must be hundreds of them,' said Ben, looking up. 'Listen, James, don't get me wrong, I've had a lovely evening, but I think it's time we left now.'

James gave a nod, but as he turned to leave, a man he at once recognised walked outside to greet Queen Abigail. Upon reaching the queen, the man knelt, his clothing darker than the night itself.

'Rise, Gilbert,' Queen Abigail ordered.

Obediently, Gilbert got to his feet.

When James clapped eyes on Gilbert, he felt sick; weak, almost. He craved revenge, but that would have to wait. Right now, Ben and Mary needed him.

The queen and Gilbert turned around and walked towards the castle doors, exchanging words as they went.

When they arrived at the threshold, they were greeted by an elderly man with a long white beard that nearly reached the ground. He was wearing a matching blue robe and pointed hat and looked like a very important figure.

The old man waited for Gilbert and they both walked through the doors together, their voices raised as though something had gone terribly wrong.

James didn't even try to hear what was being said; his main concern was getting out of the forest as quickly as possible. 'Let's get out of here!' he said, taking a couple of backward steps.

A few minutes later, the children were out of sight and James felt it would be safe to take to the sky again. 'The Dakotas won't see us now,' he explained, holding out his hands. Strangely, he felt only one of his hands being taken.

Ben beat him to the question. 'Where's Mary?'

James shrugged. 'I thought she was with you!'

Ben waved a hand in the air and cried, 'She was up front with you the last time I checked.'

'Look for her, quick.' A rustle of the leaves behind him made James turn. To his absolute horror, Mary had the unwelcome company of a Dakota; its left claw was wrapped around her waist, its right holding a sword dangerously close to her throat.

'Let her go!' James demanded, brandishing his sword.

With a fierce roar, the Dakota extended its black wings and flew into the air.

'Help, James!' Mary called out, kicking her legs furiously in an attempt to struggle free.

Without even thinking, James shot into the air and, holding his sword in his right hand, chased the Dakota through the forest, dodging trees as he flew.

Getting closer, he noticed the creature's bright red eyes glancing back at him. He knew it hadn't seen the tree that was looming in front of them. As expected, the creature slammed straight into it.

At the same time, Mary fell from the creature's grasp, gravity ensuring that she plummeted towards the ground at great speed.

James, who had almost collided with a tree, caught her, then turned in mid-air and flew back towards Ben.

The Dakota, meanwhile, shook its head, pinpointed the children's position and resumed its chase.

'Are you okay?' James shouted to Mary while he manoeuvred skilfully around trees.

'Yes – just keep flying,' cried Mary, who could now see Ben standing amongst the trees, waving his hands in a mad frenzy, willing them to go faster.

As James handed Mary over, he felt hugely relieved, but there was still work to be done as the relentless Dakota was flying straight towards him.

After taking a deep breath, he threw his sword into the air like a javelin, and watched as the weapon struck down the airborne animal.

There was a harsh series of screams, each one louder than the last.

For a moment, James thought the deafening screams of pain would never end, but then, joyously, they stopped completely. He stood still, watching the creature exhaling its last breath. He was surprised at how little pity he felt.

He walked over and retrieved his bloody sword. 'There'll be more here soon,' he said, turning and facing Ben and Mary. 'We have to leave.'

Joining hands, they flew back down the lane. When the steep drop of the mountain came into view, they sighed with relief.

Then, led by James, they ran and jumped from the mountaintop, their clothes flapping wildly in the breeze as they glided towards the magical land below.

★

In Darken Castle, Queen Abigail walked over to her throne, sat down, fixed the gold crown on her head and glared at Gilbert. 'Report,' she said flatly.

'The boy is no longer a concern,' Gilbert assured her.

The queen stared at him with her frightening eyes. 'Glad to hear that,' she said after a moment. 'And the diamond?' She paused, hoping for a positive response. 'I trust you found it?'

'I'm afraid the diamond still eludes us, Your Majesty,' Gilbert told her. 'We searched the place from top to bottom, but there was no diamond.'

Looking melancholy, the queen said, 'Tell me then, where is it?'

'I think the old man might've given it to someone in Zara,' replied Gilbert. 'I will gather the army and search Zara immediately. If they have it, I will find it.'

'Make sure you do, Gilbert,' said Abigail. 'I'm growing rather tired of waiting.'

'We all are,' said Gilbert.

The queen nodded. 'You may leave.'

'Yes, Your Majesty,' said Gilbert. After a parting bow, he left the great hall. His footsteps were still echoing around the stone walls when two black cats climbed on to the throne beside the queen, one of them jumping up on to her lap.

She ran a hand across the cat's back. Then, sensing something, she lifted the cat upwards and glared into the animal's eyes. A moment later, her face turned red and she roared, *'Gilbert!'*

★

In the Zaran forest, the children had arrived and Grampian, who had never met Ben or Mary before, greeted them warmly.

'Welcome, friends of James,' he said proudly. 'We've been expecting you. My name is Grampian and I am the leader of the orchin community in Orchestra.'

Mary liked Grampian instantly and went out of her way to introduce herself to him.

'Hello, little one,' said Grampian, extending a warm hand towards her.

James and Ben giggled. Grampian was barely taller than her.

'I am very pleased to meet you, Grampian,' said Mary eagerly, shaking his hand.

'And you must be Ben,' said Grampian. 'It's a pleasure to finally meet you.'

Ben shook Grampian's little hand and smiled.

'Now,' said Grampian with a smile, 'when you're all ready we shall begin our journey to the palace.'

'There's a palace?' pressed Mary, delighted.

'Why, yes – and quite a large one at that, too,' replied Grampian.

'Cool,' said Ben.

For once, Mary agreed with him.

Grampian took out a white whistle and blew it three times. Instantly, the whole orchin community rushed into a single file and began walking through the forest.

'Just follow the orchins and all will be well,' said Grampian, grinning from ear to ear.

Arm in arm, Ben and Mary strolled behind the orchins, while James and Grampian followed behind everyone else.

Grampian was humming a merry tune as he walked along. Suddenly, he stopped and cast an eye on James's bloodstained sword. 'I see you are learning fast.' He smiled. 'You saw Queen Abigail, didn't you?'

'No, of course not,' lied James. 'Why would you say that?'

Grampian raised his eyebrows and grinned at him knowingly.

James finally owned up. 'I did,' he said. 'I passed the water. I just had to see. Are you angry with me?'

'Not at all,' replied Grampian. 'I had a feeling you would.'

James said, 'She had a giant with her. Who is he?'

'That's not a giant.' Grampian frowned. 'It's a Volen.'

James shook his head. 'A Volen?'

'Yes, a Volen,' said Grampian. 'They might look human, but they're much closer to an animal. They can run at high speeds, but a loud humming sound vibrates from them when they do, so you can tell rather easily when they're approaching. What is really disturbing about them is their voice.'

James was lost. 'Their voice?'

'Yes, the tone of a Volen's voice is quite normal – even soothing,' remarked Grampian. 'But never be fooled: they are extremely violent animals.' He smiled at James. 'Not to worry; you won't come across another one any time soon.'

James still had another question for Grampian. 'I also saw an old man with the queen. He had a long white beard and wore a blue robe.' He looked at Grampian curiously. 'Who's he?'

Grampian's smile melted like ice in the sunshine. 'That's the sorcerer Imorex,' he said in a voice that suggested saying the name was painful on his lips. 'There's not a decision made in Darken without his counsel. However, he is a person best avoided. He has dark powers that are…' He hesitated. 'Well, let's just say, nobody really knows how he acquired them.'

'What's that supposed to mean?' asked James, deciding to press.

Grampian elaborated. 'Nobody is born a sorcerer; they don't just acquire certain powers out of nowhere. They have to find them from somewhere, and more often than not –' he paused and seemed to choose his next words very carefully, '– well, their methods of finding these powers are often unnatural.'

Confused, James shook his head, wishing he had never asked.

Once again, Grampian held one hand in the air and said strongly, 'I suggest we keep moving. It won't be long now.'

- CHAPTER THIRTY-SIX -

An Evil Plot

Judging from Queen Abigail's stern expression, Gilbert had already guessed that the news was bad.

'You lied to me,' said the queen in an aggressive tone of voice. 'You said he was dead.'

Gilbert shook his head. 'I said he was no longer a concern,' he replied calmly. 'That is still the case.'

The sorcerer Imorex entered the hall and, after lifting his robe from beneath his boots, sat down on a high-backed chair next to the queen's throne. 'I'm afraid the boy was in Darken only an hour ago.'

Gilbert faltered. 'That can't be,' he said. 'There was no way out.'

'Well, he has found a way to get here, Gilbert,' replied the queen.

Gilbert shrugged. 'Is that such a bad thing?'

The queen merely looked at him, confused.

'You wanted him here, didn't you?' Gilbert pointed out.

Queen Abigail's face darkened a little. 'Dead, Gilbert,' she replied. 'Not wandering around my kingdom.' She shot Imorex a glance. 'Do you know where he is?'

Imorex gave an ambiguous nod, then snapped his fingers. A Volen strode forward, carrying a bowl of water which he handed to the sorcerer, who then placed it carefully on a table before him. Concentrating, he covered his ears and stared into the still water.

The queen looked at Gilbert, then back at Imorex, her mood still fragile.

A moment later, the sorcerer Imorex lifted his head, water dripping from his long fringe. 'He is somewhere in Zara,' he declared. 'Where exactly, I'm not entirely sure.'

The queen moved to the edge of her throne, clearly dissatisfied with the answer. 'Well, where in Zara? The palace?'

Imorex rubbed his tired eyes. 'As far as I can tell, yes.'

'You're not sure?'

'My visions are blurred, but he is either at the palace or very close to it at least.'

Straightening the collar of his coat, Gilbert moved closer to the throne and said, 'Your Majesty, might I make a suggestion?'

'By all means.'

'I'll mount an army. Give me one hour and I'll have him located.'

As Gilbert spoke, the queen's expression had gradually softened.

'No, I have a better idea,' she said. Turning to one of the roaming cats beside her, she smiled evilly.

CHAPTER THIRTY-SEVEN

Kila

They had made it; the orchins had finally brought James home to where he truly belonged. Grampian pointed to the majestic palace before him. 'Do you remember this place, James?'

James was shaking his head. The palace was cream-coloured and made his grandfather's mansion look like a modest bungalow in comparison. It was a breathtaking sight, but not one he had any recollection of.

'Well, how could you, I suppose?' Grampian shrugged. 'You were only a baby, after all.'

Next moment, James heard the sound of the large white gates opening and a group of tall men came striding out.

'Master,' said the first man in the line, 'my name is Kila and I am the leader of the 12 knights of Zara.'

Kila was a handsome man, sallow-skinned and broad-shouldered. He was about 35 years old, very athletic and strong, with a fully grown beard and brown hair that ran to his shoulders.

James walked up the pathway towards the gates, stopping at the point where Kila stood. Only now, under the brightness of the moonlight, did he realise just how tall Kila actually was. As they shook hands, he peered upwards and said, 'So, you're a knight?'

'Yes, master.'

Kila, however, looked nothing like a knight, or how James had always imagined one would look. There was no metal armour, no silver helmet; just simple brown clothing that showed his muscular physique. He did, however, have a large belt from which hung a fine sword.

James liked to believe that one day he too might resemble Kila.

'We have waited patiently for your return, master,' declared another sturdy man.

James was cringing. 'Why are you calling me your master?'

Kila gave James a strange look. 'Because you are,' he said. 'Like your father before you.'

James shrugged, looking embarrassed. 'I'm not.'

'What should we call you, then?' asked a huge man beside Kila.

James felt like laughing. 'James will do fine,' he said with a smile.

Ben was waving his hand in the air. 'Over here! Yeah, I call him Jimbo sometimes if that's any help.'

Mary giggled.

Using his shoulder, James pushed them both forward. 'These are my friends.'

The men all nodded and smiled politely at the children.

Grampian held up a hand. 'Now then, it's been a very long day and our new friends are hungry.'

'Of course,' bellowed Kila, 'come inside.' Then he lifted Mary into his arms, exactly like Wilmore used to, and everyone followed them through the gates and into the palace.

- CHAPTER THIRTY-EIGHT -

Exploring the Palace

Inside, the Zaran palace sparkled with gold. The doors, the floors and even the four chandeliers dangling regally overhead seemed to be made from the precious metal.

After walking through a magnificent archway, the children followed Grampian and the 12 knights into what appeared to be a dining chamber, although Mary thought it looked more like a ballroom.

The whole hall was surrounded by magnificent tapestries and a long glass table, set for at least 50, ran down the middle of the chamber.

The children walked quietly over to the table, sat down on the high chairs and kept their heads bowed, only peering up occasionally to glance at one another.

A moment later, at least 20 orchins entered from a side door carrying heavy trays which they were struggling to control.

The children were famished. For the next half an hour, they gratefully consumed all the food that was produced to them. It was like a banquet: the cutlery was gold, the goblets were embellished with jewels and the silver trays were piled high with piping-hot food.

When everybody's hunger was satisfied, Kila lifted his goblet, rose to his feet and proposed a toast.

The chamber fell silent.

'People of Zara,' Kila began, 'we may be few in number, but today we've found our king.'

The knights cheered.

'11 years ago,' Kila went on, 'many a man lost his life for the sake of our saviour. Those brave men died so that we would see this day.' With a broad smile, he held his goblet up a little higher, spilling some wine in the process. 'My friends, today will always be remembered as the day James Clyde returned home.'

The man beside Kila got up from his chair first. 'Well spoken,' the man cried, clapping loudly.

The orchins, along with the remaining knights, stood upright and added to the applause whilst keeping their eyes on James.

Feeling hugely embarrassed, James stared at the half-eaten chunk of meat sitting on his plate until the applause stopped a few minutes later.

Overwhelmed, he finally looked up, only to observe Ben and Mary smiling at him. His intuition told him that Mary was very proud, while he also got the impression that Ben was taking great delight in his embarrassment.

When all the speeches were finished, the children were shown to their bed chamber by Grampian, who guided them up the grand staircase and through several winding corridors before finally stopping at a part of the palace that he referred to as "the west wing".

'It's the next chamber on the left.' Grampian tapped Mary on the shoulder and pointed to the door. 'Would you like to go in first?'

Accepting the invitation, Mary placed her hand on the golden handle and, using all her strength, pushed the door open. Stepping quickly inside, she could hardly believe it.

Ben peered in next and then James, who looked equally as surprised.

The chamber was uncannily similar to their old bedroom at Wilmore Clyde's house: three luxurious beds, tables positioned in the same locations and wide-open balcony doors beside the last bed, affording them a splendid view of Orchestra. *A replica.*

Walking further inside, James felt as though he had returned to his old house and half expected his grandfather to greet him at any moment. He stood still, looking around, unable to ignore the resemblance.

At that moment, three more orchins came quietly into the chamber, all holding different items of James's pyjamas, which looked like they had been washed and neatly ironed.

'Where did you get those?' asked James.

'We have our ways,' replied Grampian. 'Now then, I'll see you all in the morning.' He turned to leave, then stopped. 'By the way, James, your training starts tomorrow, so make sure you get a good night's sleep. You'll need it.'

'That doesn't sound good,' said James in a serious tone of voice.

'Well,' said Grampian, 'you will be going into combat with the greatest swordsman that has ever lived in Orchestra.'

Ben, yawning, said, 'Who would that be?'

'Kila,' declared Grampian with pride. 'Truly a master of his art, but anyway, that's for tomorrow. Tonight, get your rest.' He nodded politely before walking from the chamber.

'I'm exhausted,' cried Ben, throwing himself on to his bed.

'Me too,' said Mary, getting into her bed and pulling the blankets up over herself. 'Goodnight, James.'

'Goodnight, Mary.'

'Goodnight,' Mary muttered back, fighting to keep her eyes open.

'Yeah, goodnight, master,' said Ben, laughing, enjoying the moment. Then, walking over to a goblet sitting on a tray, he hoisted it into the air.

James shook his head, trying hard not to smile. 'What are you doing, you idiot?'

Keeping his eyes focused on the goblet held aloft in his right hand and with his expression deadly serious, Ben imitated the scene from earlier in the dining chamber. 'Today our king has returned!' he said, mustering the deepest voice he could. '11 long years we have waited!'

James's lips slowly curled into a smile. 'About time you knew who the boss was around here!'

Several minutes later, as the children lay in their beds, Ben asked James a question. 'Why does my nose feel really strange since I've stopped wearing glasses?'

James groaned. 'Gosh, let me think about that one and I'll get back to you. So you can see perfectly, then?'

'Pretty much, yeah.'

'And how do you reckon that happened?'

'Beats me.'

'Can I ask you a question?'

'Fire away.'

James sat up. 'What do you think of Orchestra?'

Ben paused, uncertain how to answer. 'Some parts are beautiful, but others are just plain creepy.' He glanced across at Mary's bed. 'What do you reckon, blondie?'

There was no response.

'Blondie?'

'She's fast asleep,' whispered James.

'It has been a long day,' Ben whispered back, yawning, his eyelids now barely open.

'I suppose,' said James, 'but I'm just too excited to sleep.' He smiled over at Ben. 'Aren't you?'

James cocked his ear, hoping for a similar response, but instead all he got were tired grunts and ill-tempered mutterings of good night, which sounded more like code names for "keep quiet!".

To pass the time, he looked around the chamber. Again, he couldn't help noticing the resemblance between this room and the one at his grandfather's house. Just thinking of his beloved grandfather made him feel like burying his head in his pillow and crying for the rest of the night.

As he turned restlessly in his bed, he arrived at the conclusion that he just couldn't sleep, nor would he any time soon. As far as he was concerned, he had to leave this chamber immediately.

Sitting up, he decided it was high time that he explored the palace.

CHAPTER THIRTY-NINE

Hope

James, now attired in his blue and white striped pyjamas, crept from his chamber, travelled down several flights of stairs and slipped into the elegant dining chamber where he had been only hours earlier.

Standing still, he peered around. Given the late hour, the chamber was suitably dark and quiet. He felt desperately disappointed. What should he do now?

Going back to his chamber and lying in bed whilst reminiscing about everything that had happened was simply not an option, but he still had to find something to do.

It was then that a harsh cough broke the silence.

James looked everywhere. Unless he was mistaken, the cough seemed to have come from the long table. He frowned. *Nobody's there.*

Heading quickly forward, there was now adequate moonlight to see a single person sitting at the table. He recognised the figure instantly.

It was Kila.

He moved closer to the table, like a nervous schoolboy approaching the headmaster's desk. How should he make Kila aware of his presence?

Should he simply say, 'Kila!'?

Tap a shoulder?

Cough?

By the light of the moons, he could see a goblet of wine and a gleaming sword resting beside Kila's hand.

Before he could take another step, Kila said, without turning his head, 'Hello, James Clyde.'

James walked forward, facing Kila now. 'You knew I was here?'

'Since the moment you were at the top of the stairs.' Kila beamed a smile as he pulled out a chair. 'Please, take a seat.'

As James sat down, Kila said, 'Can you not sleep?'

'Nope,' replied James. 'I wish I could, though. Can you not?'

Kila heaved a troubled sigh. 'Unfortunately, I have a good deal on my mind – as do you, I suspect.'

James nodded sheepishly.

Kila smiled, then reached for the red wine.

'Did you know my father, Kila?' asked James.

Kila set the goblet back on the table. 'Your father, yes. I knew him very well.'

James thought he detected a touch of sadness in Kila's voice.

'He was my king,' Kila went on, 'but also my good friend.' After swallowing another mouthful of wine, he looked at James with intent. 'Are you ready to follow in his footsteps?'

'Er, I don't know.' James paused, looking at Kila. 'Am I really the King of Zara?'

Kila gave a nod. 'Yes, you are, but you've much to learn – let's not put any titles on you just yet.'

James was relieved; he didn't want the pressure of being a king and he most certainly didn't feel like royalty. 'Kila, I need to know one thing about my father –'

'Anything.'

'Who killed him?' James hesitated, wondering if he should be asking these questions. 'Was it Queen Abigail?'

James saw sadness when he looked into Kila's eyes. He was certain he had overstepped the mark with this question, but it was his father and he had a right to know.

Kila shook his head. 'No, it wasn't Abigail. She played her part and ordered the assassination, but she didn't actually kill him.'

'Then who did?'

Kila sat up. 'We had the best army in the land and they had no way of getting to our king, but we were betrayed. One of the most respected knights in Zara went into your father's chamber and poisoned his drink.'

James suddenly had a sinking feeling. 'What was the knight's name?'

'Gilbert,' said Kila, looking directly at James, whose head dropped instantly.

Kila's eyes narrowed. 'You know him?'

James nodded solemnly. 'He killed my grandfather, too.'

Kila put a hand on James's shoulder.

James raised his head and looked back at him. 'Why have I been brought to Orchestra?' he cried. 'Please tell me the truth. I'm 11 years old. I am not a warrior or a king. What could I do to help?'

Kila smiled. 'More than you could possibly know right now.'

'What does that mean?' Looking up, James suddenly noticed a more serious expression upon Kila's face.

'James, perhaps one day I will bring you to the mass graves at the far side of the kingdom. Maybe then you will realise what this land has been through. This world needs somebody; this land needs hope. You're that great hope – whether you like it or not.'

James remained silent for a few seconds, then said, 'Will you help me?'

Kila stood up slowly. 'You don't even have to ask,' he said, holding out the large palm of his hand. 'You have my complete loyalty.'

After shaking Kila's hand, James found himself looking at the sword lying across the table. He knew this sword had probably taken countless lives and it fascinated him.

'Impressive, isn't it?' said Kila, noticing James's wandering eye.

Nodding, James placed his hand on the blade.

Kila went on, 'You want revenge, James, and you will get it. Let's take one step at a time.'

James frowned. 'Kila, would you be disappointed in me if I told you I was frightened?'

'I would be worried if you weren't,' replied Kila. 'Tomorrow, however, I will show you how to handle a sword and you will find out for yourself that you have nothing to be frightened about.' He sat back down on his chair and pointed to the grand staircase. 'You should try and get some sleep.'

James walked towards the grand staircase, then turned to face Kila once more. 'Did you know my mother?'

Kila nodded. 'I did. She was a wonderful woman and would've been a great mother.' He smiled kindly. 'She loved you dearly.'

'Are the rumours true?' persisted James. 'Is she still alive?'

Standing up, Kila looked James in the eye. 'I honestly don't know,' he said. 'Some people say she is, while others think that she isn't. What matters though is what you think. What does your heart tell you?'

James smiled knowingly, then climbed the stairs.

★

Although he got lost once or twice, he finally made it back to his chamber, tiredness now overpowering him. The balcony doors rattled in the wind and the white curtains billowed like two ghosts dancing with one another.

He glanced over at Ben and Mary, who had never looked happier as they slept peacefully in their beds.

Trying to be discreet, he tiptoed across the chamber. As he prepared to shut the doors, however, something brushed against his arm, causing him to jump.

Peering into the darkness, he saw two yellow eyes, like headlights in the night, staring back at him from close range.

The black cat looked straight at him, gave a vicious meow, then ran along, disappearing into the night.

James naturally thought nothing off it. With all his might, he closed the doors and climbed into bed.

CHAPTER FORTY

Darken Prepares for Battle

The cat hurried through the Darken forest, scampering over branches with ease along the way. It squeezed through the gates, under the queen's carriage and into the castle's great hall.

Sensing something immediately, Queen Abigail picked the cat up, stared long and hard into the animal's eyes and saw the face of a young boy, presumably James Clyde, staring back at her from inside a palace chamber. Turning to the sorcerer Imorex beside her, she said loudly, 'He is here. Am I too late?'

'The son of the king is still a boy and not a man as prophesied,' Imorex told her. 'It's not too late, but we must act quickly.'

The queen nodded. 'Get Gilbert.'

★

In the lowest level of the castle, Gilbert moved a lantern from side to side, checking the many dungeons surrounding him. He held a handkerchief to his nose, trying to combat the foul smell in the air.

Arriving at the last dungeon in the row, he raised the lantern and illuminated the cell. 'After all these years, we finally have a use for you.'

As he slid a key into the cell lock, he felt a hand on his shoulder. He turned and saw the massive form of a Volen standing before him.

The Volen whispered in his ear.

Wasting no time, Gilbert pocketed the key and dashed back along the corridor.

Entering the great hall moments later, he knelt.

'Rise, Gilbert,' ordered Queen Abigail, waving him up.

'You wished to see me, Your Majesty?' said Gilbert, rising to his feet.

'Yes, Gilbert,' said the queen resolutely. 'The boy is at the Zaran palace. Round up the entire army and get the weapons prepared.' She took a deep breath. 'We charge tomorrow!'

- CHAPTER FORTY-ONE -

Mentor Versus Pupil

James Clyde awoke slowly, puzzled by his strange surroundings. Then, like remembering a vague dream, it all came back to him. *Kila, Gilbert, and the diamonds of Orchestra.*

Grampian was standing in the chamber, the stem of his tall red hat the only part of him visible at the foot of the bed.

James yawned. 'What time is it? Hold on, do you even *have* time here?'

Grampian moved across the chamber, lifted James's white boots from under a chair and brought them back towards the bed. 'Yes, we measure time, much like the other world.'

'Good. Just five more minutes, then,' pleaded James, turning over.

'No, it's already late morning. Kila is waiting for you.'

'Two more minutes, then.'

Grampian was shaking his head. 'Sorry, it's time to get up!'

James sighed, but he knew Grampian was right. Being late for his first lesson wasn't a good idea. Slowly, with one eye open, he got up from his bed.

After a late breakfast, Grampian guided James to the back of the palace, where they entered a wide courtyard that was flanked by luscious gardens and graced with stunning flowerbeds.

Returning his focus back to the courtyard, James now saw Kila, who was accompanied by his 11 knights.

'Good morning, James,' said Kila. 'Are you ready to learn?'

James gave a tired smile.

Kila laughed. 'I'll take that as a yes.' Using the tip of his sword, he pointed towards the line of men on his right. 'I would like you to meet my friends.'

He began the introductions with a bright smile. 'This is Joseph, the best man with a bow and arrow in the kingdom.' He quickly introduced the rest of the men, slapping each of them on the arm as he walked past. 'This is Eric, next is Ethan, then David, Gabriel, Joel, Lance, Noah, Matthew, Nathan. And the last man in the line is Tobias.'

As James travelled further along the line, he noticed that the knights were getting taller and the one thing that struck him above anything else was how big their hands were – at least twice the size of his own.

Kila was smiling. 'Trust these men as you would trust me. They have all bled for me.'

All of a sudden, the 11 knights retreated and formed a circle around Kila and James.

'Now, take out your sword and fight me,' cried Kila, his mood suddenly darkening.

James hoped he had heard wrong. 'Huh? I can't fight yet.'

'How do you know you can't?' replied Kila. 'You haven't tried.'

James shook his head. 'I'm still pretty sure.'

'Come now,' said Kila.

Tentatively, James drew his gold sword and clasped the hilt with both hands. Then he looked around. The courtyard looked more like a Roman Coliseum. He had no idea how he could match Kila in such an arena. Still, he had a feeling Kila had been teasing him. He knew perfectly well that he would have to learn the basics first.

Wrong!

Not holding back, Kila attacked, swinging his sword two-handed at James.

That can't be good, James thought, taking a step back. Reacting on instinct, he held up his sword and, to his utter amazement, blocked Kila's blade from connecting.

Kila withdrew his sword, took two quick steps forward and swung again.

Once more, James warded this off. Then, gaining confidence, he flashed his own sword.

Steel clashed.

Sparks flew.

Swords criss-crossed.

'Enough,' shouted Kila minutes later, placing his sword by his side.

Gasping for breath, James looked at his sword. 'How can I fight like that? Is it this sword?'

'How does a bird fly, James?'

James nearly laughed, but thought twice when he saw the serious expression on Kila's face. 'It uses its wings.'

'And its instinct,' added Kila. 'Don't forget, you were born for this.'

James shrugged. 'Maybe.'

Kila raised his eyebrows. 'Maybe?'

'Okay, probably.'

Kila frowned. 'Probably?'

James laughed and said, 'Okay! I was born for this.'

'Better!' Kila lifted his sword, walked towards James and prepared to restart the fight. 'Ready?'

James looked at his sword, like a child desperate to play with a new toy. 'Ready,' he said strongly, tipping Kila's sword with his own.

They began again.

★

James's attitude was veering towards cavalier as he dashed all over the courtyard like a veteran of the sword. Showing where their allegiance lay, the 11 knights cheered his every move.

Showing no fear, James swung violently at Kila's shoulder and connected, sending blood shooting to the ground, which smeared the white stone. Stopping, he held a hand over his mouth. *What have I done?*

Kila looked at his ripped clothes, then back at James. 'I thought you couldn't fight?' he said, raising his eyebrows. 'Again!'

'Let's go,' said James.

A quick flick of Kila's sword gave him a slight advantage.

James retreated but recovered well, countering with a quick trust of his own blade.

Kila parried it, then attacked with a riposte.

James fended off this new approach, retreated, then attacked with a riposte of his own. He missed – but only just.

Kila smiled, enjoying the contest.

James dashed to the side, trying to figure out Kila's weakness. Did Kila even have any? He bided his time, trying to stay with Kila's relentless speed, but his sword was starting to feel heavy; it was like he was holding a tonne weight.

'Your wrist is getting weak, isn't it?' shouted Kila.

James pushed Kila on to the back foot. *Are you reading my mind?* 'No, what makes you think that?'

'I can feel it.'

'Oh, really?'

'It's nothing to be ashamed about. You're very talented – brilliant, even – but you're not a master.'

James cut his sword through the air and said, through gritted teeth, 'What's the difference?'

Kila took two steps back and placed his sword by his side. 'My father once told me that a good swordsman eventually tires, but a master doesn't.'

James moved forward, shaking his head. 'And I suppose you're a master.'

Kila gave a mischievous smile. 'Well…'

CHAPTER FORTY-TWO

Kila's Childhood

Kila was a master; there was no doubt about that.

His mastery of the sword, however, hadn't happened overnight. It took strict dedication and over 10 years of devoted practice to achieve the title of master.

As a child, his day consisted of rising at dawn and fencing with his father, who was also a great swordsman.

But *not* a master.

Kila knew his father was passionate about sword fighting. At meals, his father would discuss tactics with him: how to counteract different moves that might be used by an opponent. He was schooled in the art of attack, but also the science behind a good defence.

As he fought James, Kila's mind drifted elsewhere – he was with his father again, standing in a deserted courtyard, the moonlight shining on him.

He was 12 years old, lifting large rocks with his hands, his father beside him, urging him to increase his speed. *'Faster, boy, faster!'*

The young Kila tried, but his hands suddenly began to drip blood. With a groan, he let the blood-smeared rocks fall and brought his hands to his eyes, studying his fingers closely.

'Papa, I'm bleeding!'

'So you are,' replied his father. 'And?'

'I think I've had enough, don't you? Everyone else is in bed.' Kila turned to leave.

'Where are you going?' His father sounded more disappointed than angry.

'Inside!' said Kila, and he began to walk towards the palace.

There was a brief silence.

'Son,' his father called out.

Head down, Kila kept walking.

'My beloved son!'

Kila turned, annoyed. 'What?'

'Don't you want to be the best?' his father asked him.

Sighing, Kila threw his arms in the air. *Wasn't it obvious?* 'Of course I do,' he said, suddenly realising he was shouting. 'But it's all the time, papa! If I'm not reading about swords, I'm using one. It's too much.'

'Kila, being the best often means you have to make sacrifices.' He walked towards Kila, taking tentative steps. 'I'm not a master, Kila, but you could be. You don't realise it now, but one day you will – being a master will save your life. You will be a yard faster than your adversary, a fraction quicker in reacting. You will have an advantage over everyone.' He placed his hands on Kila's shoulders and looked down at him. 'But son… Look at me, son.'

Kila looked up, his eyes tearful.

'It's your own choice. I would never make you do anything against your will.' His father smiled kindly at him and wiped away a tear.

Kila didn't smile back; he looked down at his hands and noticed that the blood was still oozing. This surprised him: he could feel nothing. He walked past his father, gathered the two rocks and started working on his arms.

Years later, when his father died of old age, Kila placed one of the rocks stained with dried blood on the grave. The other rock was in a casket in his chamber. It dominated the entire room and every now and then Kila would open the casket and look at it – admire it.

Not only was the rock a reminder of his father, but also of the work he had had to endure to become the man he was today.

Weeks after his father's funeral, Kila was declared a master and in the years that followed nobody had ever come close to defeating him – until now.

This morning, an 11-year-old boy with no experience of the sword was pushing him to the brink, testing him like no knight, Dakota or Volen ever had.

However, the outcome of the duel was still in the balance.

Kila emerged from his dream and decided to deliver the onslaught. Without delay, he increased the power and intensity of his blade.

This had an immediate effect.

James had hesitated in adjusting to the new speed of the fight. It was a very slight pause – only a split second – but to Kila it was more than enough.

To a master, it was an opening. A chance.

Taking advantage, Kila wrapped his hands around the handle of his sword and struck.

James felt the strength leave his hand and an electric current travelled up the length of his arm, such was the force of the blow. Trembling, he tried to fight back, but the momentum of the fight had changed.

One more strike and James was on the back foot.

The next strike sent his sword flying from his hand.

The final strike put him on his knees.

Quickly, he fumbled to retrieve his sword, but it was too late.

The tall, broad figure of Kila paced nonchalantly forward.

Sprawled on the ground, James knew the fight was over. Or was it? Suddenly, an idea popped into his head.

'Do you surrender?' asked Kila, his sword pointed forward and aimed at James's throat.

James looked up defiantly. 'Never!' He exploded off the ground, somersaulted over Kila's head, lifted his sword and pressed it strongly into Kila's spine.

The assembled crowd erupted.

James now asked Kila the same question. 'Do you surrender?'

Kila felt the steel pressed firmly into the base of his spine. Turning fully around, he looked at James with pride. 'I've never fought a person who could fly before.'

The round of applause that followed was deafening. As it continued, the 11 knights rushed towards James. Gabriel, Joel and Lance were the first to shake his hand and offer words of congratulations.

'Now you will start to believe,' said Gabriel, crushing James's hand.

'If you can defeat Kila, you can defeat anyone,' insisted Lance, smiling proudly as he patted James on the shoulder.

Ben Forester, who had awoken to sounds of steel clashing minutes earlier, was now looking at James intently. 'How can you fight like that?'

James shook his head. 'No idea!' He raised his sword and looked at it. 'But I'd say it has something to do with this.'

Kila sensed Ben's eagerness. 'Not to worry, young Ben. You will learn one day, too.'

The gentle breeze wafted the smell of food from the kitchens, and Kila patted his firm stomach. 'Well now, all this running around has given me an appetite.'

'Just a moment,' said Joseph, his eyes turning to James. 'Have you ever done archery before?'

'Done what?' asked James.

'Used a bow and arrow before,' explained Joseph.

'Er, no,' muttered James.

Joseph smiled. 'Good, you will learn then,' he said. 'Follow us.' He glanced at Kila. 'Unless, of course, you've a problem with that?'

'Of course not,' replied Kila, 'but the boy must be getting hungry.'

'Oh, I'm not too bad, Kila.' James swished his sword through the air. 'Besides, I've always wanted to use a bow and arrow.'

'Well then, you've chosen the right moment,' said Kila. 'You couldn't learn from a better man. As I've already said, Joseph's the best there is.'

All the knights apart from Kila walked with James past the curtain wall and into another courtyard.

Kila watched as they passed from his sight. Touching the gash on his shoulder, he winced.

'I'll have a look at that, if you like?' said Grampian, noticing the blood beginning to drip.

Kila downplayed it. 'No, it's just a scratch.' He spat on his sleeve and dabbed the cloth over the wound. 'Besides, the scar will be a souvenir from the day James Clyde learnt the sword.'

Ben looked high up at Kila's shoulder and studied the wound. He shivered.

Kila smiled at him. 'These things can appear worse than they are.' He rested a hand on Ben's shoulder. 'Come along, Ben. You can eat James's share.'

- CHAPTER FORTY-THREE -

Tell Me Everything

James surveyed the courtyard. Archery boards, about three metres apart, ran in a line against the adjacent wall. To his left, bows hung on a rack. A nearby wooden table was stacked with arrows.

Joseph lifted an arrow and studied it like a surgeon studying a scalpel. He pointed the tip of the arrow towards an archery board. 'We'll be using that one.' He made final adjustments to his stance. 'I will hit the middle circle.' Breathing calmly, he angled and fired.

The arrow whistled through the air and, as predicted, split the middle of the board.

A bullseye!

A round of applause went up.

James was clapping louder than anybody else. 'That was amazing,' he said, looking up at Joseph.

'Thanks.' Joseph passed James the bow. He took an arrow from his shoulder strap, handed it to James and said, 'The most important aspects of archery are accuracy and technique. You must at all times hit your target and the key to doing that is through good concentration.'

James held the bow and arrow like any untutored person would: grip tight on the bow, fingers limp on the arrow and elbows overly bent. He smiled to himself. Even flying for the first time hadn't been as tricky as this.

He placed the arrow clumsily on the string of the bow, took a quick glance at the board, closed one eye and fired.

The arrow zigzagged through the air before lodging harmlessly in the grass beside the archery board.

'Keep at it, James,' said Lance. 'We have all the arrows in Orchestra and you can use every last one.'

'We'll be back in an hour or so,' announced Ethan, who, along with some of the other knights, walked back into the palace, muttering about how hungry they were.

James, meanwhile, stayed outside, now clearly hooked on archery as he fired arrow after arrow.

Trying to concentrate with everyone watching closely was tough, but he did his best; he persevered and was now visibly improving. His body alignment was much better, he followed through on the release of the arrow and his bow arm was a lot steadier.

Nathan glanced at Joseph. 'The boy has potential.'

'And a great willingness to learn,' remarked Tobias, stroking his clean-shaven chin ponderously.

Joseph didn't speak, but simply kept his eyes fixed on James, who had just fired an arrow agonisingly close to the middle circle.

After an hour of practice, Joseph went to James and patted him on the back. 'Well done,' he said. 'You're improving.'

As they talked, Nathan walked over and beckoned James towards the table, where Tobias was already sitting as if in preparation for a meeting.

James placed the bow on the ground, walked over to the table, sat down and gazed up at the knights, who seemed to be looking at him strangely. The table, which had been stacked with arrows, was now cleared.

Joseph sat down. 'James, we have to speak to you about something of the utmost importance. All of us here and the rest of the knights who aren't have agreed that you deserve to know the truth about your father and mother and what happened to them.

Has anyone ever told you about it before?'

James nodded, his eyes searching the knights' faces. 'Well, yes actually. Kila told me about it last night.'

The knights glanced at one another.

'What did he tell you?' said Nathan, pressing.

James shrugged. 'Well, he told me that Gilbert used to be a knight of Zara.'

Joseph nodded. 'Is that all?'

'Nope,' said James, 'I also found out that Gilbert poisoned my father.'

'Anything else?' asked Joseph, raising one eyebrow.

James shook his head. Beyond that, he knew little else.

The knights swapped looks as if to suggest something had been left out. Something important.

Joseph nodded and said, 'In essence, you are correct. Your father was indeed poisoned by Gilbert, but we feel that you should know the entire story.'

'Okay,' said James, anxiously.

Casting his mind back to the past, Joseph took a deep breath, then continued with the story. '11 years ago, the land was peaceful. At that time, Gilbert was one of us. He was a respected, trusted and quite frankly revered knight of Zara. To Kila, Gilbert was more than just a mentor – he was like a brother.'

'That is what makes this story so shocking,' interrupted Tobias.

'Your father,' added Nathan, 'had been suspicious about Gilbert for some time, but Kila wouldn't hear of it.'

'His trust in Gilbert,' said Joseph, 'led to your father's death and it gives me no pleasure to tell you that James, but I must. The first sign of trouble came when King Epson of Darken died in mysterious circumstances. It was never proven, but it is widely known and accepted that he was killed by his wife, Abigail.'

James was nodding.

'You know this part, then?' said Joseph.

'Yes,' replied James. 'My granddad told me about it once.

Abigail inherited the kingdom because she wanted to search for the diamond. Then she needed control over Zara to check the other half of Orchestra.'

'Precisely,' said Joseph. 'A bloody and bitter war began between Zara and Darken.'

James knew all this and, while he listened, he found himself wondering where this story was headed. There still must be something he hadn't heard, otherwise the knights wouldn't have sat him down and started explaining everything to him from the beginning.

'This, James, is where you come in,' said Joseph suddenly.

James jumped, forgetting he had a role to play in this absorbing story. 'Me?'

'Your birth had been foretold for centuries in this land,' said Joseph. 'The legend prophesied that, with the help of the diamonds, the son of Jacob would free the people of Orchestra, conquer evil and rule over the entire land.'

Tobias was shaking his head. 'Like everybody else, we all thought the legends were myths, but Abigail clearly didn't. Once she found a diamond in the land at Darken, she was convinced the prophecies about King Jacob's son were also true.'

'So she had my father killed.'

Joseph nodded sadly. 'When your father heard a diamond had been found in the Darken forest, he had the forest in Zara checked and, after a long search, two precious diamonds were found deep beneath the ground. They were brought to a safe location, the whereabouts of which only those closest to King Jacob knew.'

'Did Gilbert know?'

'I'm afraid he did,' replied Joseph.

Tobias said, 'Under orders, we told Gilbert that we had found only one diamond in the land and that we were still searching for the second one. We hid each of the diamonds in different locations and, as far as Gilbert knew, we only had one.'

'Queen Abigail of Darken,' said Joseph, 'knew we had

discovered a diamond and there was only one way for her to get it –'

'She needed an insider,' said James.

Joseph gave a nod. 'Right again.'

James frowned. 'Gilbert?'

'Yes, Gilbert.' Joseph shook his head. 'It's not known why Gilbert turned towards Darken, as he had always been a loyal servant to the king, but there was a bizarre change in his behaviour that prompted King Jacob to question his commitment to Zara and their war against Darken. It all came to a head 11 years ago.'

James was now hooked on the story and he wanted to know exactly what had happened on that night. He wanted to know about Gilbert's betrayal, his own escape and everything leading up to that moment. 'Please tell me about it!' he demanded urgently.

'Very well,' Joseph agreed, 'but it's not a pleasant story.'

'I need to know what happened to my father,' persisted James. 'Please tell me everything.'

Joseph raised his eyebrows. 'You're sure? You want to know everything?'

James looked determined. 'Tell me everything!'

CHAPTER FORTY-FOUR

History of Orchestra

Joseph sighed deeply. Then he began the tale that James had wanted so badly to hear. He told of how Kila had approached Gilbert late one evening in the palace...

★

'Gilbert, I swear I saw it again tonight,' cried Kila.

Gilbert shook his head. 'Impossible. I've searched everywhere. These strange beings you speak of don't exist.'

'What have you seen, Kila?' Eric called out.

'Giant creatures, the size of a man, flying over Darken.'

All the knights tried to stifle their laughter.

'Are you sure you haven't drunk too much wine, old friend?' said David. He looked across at Joseph, who was standing beside a window at the far side of the chamber. 'Joseph, come and sit down. You're making me nervous.'

Joseph turned. 'The moons are evil tonight.'

David heaved a sigh. 'Well, they look the same to me,' he said haughtily. He took a mouthful of wine but spat it out as he was laughing so hard. 'Honestly, evil moons and giant creatures.'

'David, I know what I saw!' cried Kila.

Looking at Kila, Gilbert said, 'I'll search the land again with you tomorrow.'

Kila nodded, grateful for the support.

Gilbert drained his goblet and said loudly, 'Well, I'm off.' Then he walked towards the grand staircase in an anxious manner.

Kila, who sensed something was amiss, brought Gilbert to one side. 'Is everything alright?'

Gilbert's eyes narrowed inquisitively.

'You don't seem yourself tonight.' Kila had lied there; he had sensed an air of uneasiness about Gilbert since morning.

Gilbert stared into Kila's eyes, as if he wanted to share something, but then seemed to reconsider. 'I'm fine,' he said, managing a smile, 'just tired.'

Kila gave a sympathetic smile. 'Get a good night's sleep. I'll talk to you in the morning.'

As Gilbert ascended the stairs, Kila went back to the table, sat down and poured himself a goblet of wine.

When Gilbert had passed from sight and his footsteps no longer echoed around the chamber, the knights looked at one another with expressions of suspicion and distrust.

'Keep an eye on him,' said Joseph, looking at Noah, who waited a second and then followed Gilbert up the stairs.

Although Kila knew some of the knights had been questioning Gilbert's loyalty to the cause, he was still stung by the suddenness of their actions. 'Wait, Noah,' he shouted, getting up from his chair. 'Come back here right now. Have you all lost your senses?'

'Don't let your feelings get in the way, Kila,' said Noah. 'Something isn't right here.'

'What are you insinuating?'

Noah suddenly looked very angry. 'I'm not insinuating anything, Kila. I'm telling you, we can't trust him.'

Kila looked around the chamber. 'Does everyone feel this way?' The silence that followed told him everything he needed to know. 'After all he's done for you,' he said obstinately. 'You've all got it very wrong.'

Noah shrugged. 'Anybody is capable of betrayal. What makes you so sure?'

'Do you trust me?' asked Kila.

'Of course,' replied Noah.

'Then trust Gilbert.'

Noah shook his head before continuing on his way. 'Sorry. My orders come from the king.'

'Very well,' said Kila. In a very bad temper, he followed Noah up the stairs. Before he had reached the top, however, he felt a firm hand on his elbow. He turned quickly and saw Joseph peering back.

'Kila, my respect for you is endless, but you have to admit that Gilbert's behaviour has been strange to say the least. He has been seen by people of Zara leaving the palace late at night and walking towards Darken. We have every reason to be suspicious.'

'No, you have every reason to trust him, Joseph,' Kila shouted back. 'I thought you of all people would. I mean, do you honestly believe Gilbert's a traitor?'

'I do.'

'Well then,' said Kila, 'you could not be more wrong.' And with that, he pulled his arm from Joseph's grasp and made his way up the stairs.

★

Inside the great chamber, King Jacob had just removed the crown from his head and was sitting reflectively on his throne when two firm knocks on the door broke his concentration. He sighed, then shouted, 'Enter!'

The door creaked open and Kila came walking in with his arms behind his back. Then, bowing his head, he knelt reverentially.

The king stood up from his throne and said, with a deep sigh, 'You're here about Gilbert.'

Kila rose. 'Yes I am. Is it true you have Noah following him?'

'It gives me no pleasure, but I have my reasons.'

Kila shrugged. 'What reasons?'

'I fear he is turning on us.'

'Now, why would he do that?'

'Why does anyone turn to evil?' King Jacob replied. 'Your guess is as good as mine.'

Kila looked crestfallen. 'Do you have any proof, Your Majesty?'

'Not as yet,' replied King Jacob, 'but I've given him a key to one of the diamonds.'

'You're testing him?'

'I am. If he is to betray me, it will be for a diamond.'

'You can trust him, Your Majesty,' said Kila. 'The diamond is safe in his care.'

King Jacob nodded. 'I hope you're right.' He produced a long gold key from his pocket. 'However, what he doesn't know is that I have the key to the other diamond.'

Kila sighed. *Gilbert, a traitor?* The thought was absurd. He felt like telling the king just that, but he knew he had to show a degree of reverence. Before he could protest, the king said, 'You think I'm making a mistake, don't you?'

'I feel you're being hasty, yes,' said Kila. 'We're living in paranoid times, Your Majesty. Give me a chance to speak with him. I know he will confide in me.'

The king stroked his chin. 'As you wish, Kila,' he said, reluctantly.

'Thank you, Your Majesty. This will all be cleared up before the night is over.'

'I hope you're right,' said King Jacob, 'but please be careful.'

After a quick bow, Kila walked from the great chamber, closing the thick door quietly behind him as he left.

★

Five corridors away, the knight called Gilbert sat silently on his bed, his head hung, his mind muddled. For weeks now, he had barely slept or ate, thinking about this night, which had been planned meticulously for months.

His chamber was dark with only a single candle burning on an adjacent stove. A long gold key rested on his lap.

Over and over again, he had weighed up his options. History, he knew, would not judge him kindly. Years from now, he would be portrayed as the betrayer. The man who divided the land. The man responsible for the inevitable war that would follow his actions tonight.

And yet, he looked on it differently.

He was saving the land; giving everyone a fresh start.

Just then, there were three loud and forceful knocks on his chamber door. Quickly, he stood up and the key fell from his lap, landing with a loud ding on the floor. Lifting the key, he moved closer to the door. 'Who's there?'

The voice that responded sounded agitated. 'Open up, Gilbert. We need to talk.'

CHAPTER FORTY-FIVE

The Disguise

Gilbert reacted quickly; he hurried across the chamber to a wardrobe and slipped the key into the pocket of a long black cloak that was hanging up.

No sooner had he done this than two more knocks sounded. Sweating now, he rushed back to the door and opened it. He had expected to see Kila, but instead he found himself looking at Noah. 'Is everything alright?'

'Yes. I'm sorry for the intrusion, Gilbert, but Kila wants to speak to you.'

'Now?'

'Yes, now! Is that a problem?'

Gilbert suddenly felt faint. Meeting Kila was simply out of the question. If ever he had to sound convincing, it was now. 'Yes it is,' he said. 'It's late and I'm feeling rather unwell. I think I might be coming down with something.'

Noah pointed a finger forward. 'You're sweating,' he said, calmly.

Gilbert ran a hand across his brow. 'Indeed. As you can see, I have developed a fever. Perhaps you could tell Kila that I'll speak to him first thing in the morning.'

Without breaking eye contact, Noah said, 'I'm sure he'll understand.'

'I'm sure he will.' Gilbert closed the door emphatically. The appearance of Noah had only added to his anxiety. He knew he didn't have much time.

Without delay, he went to the wardrobe, took from it the black cloak and laid it out on the bed.

This was his anonymity.

This was his disguise.

CHAPTER FORTY-SIX

Long Live King Jacob

Gilbert had always hated the white marble statue of King Jacob that adorned his chamber. On the plinth below the effigy were the words LONG LIVE KING JACOB OF ZARA.

Having donned his hooded cloak, Gilbert bent down and pushed his shoulder against the statue. Slowly it began to move, revealing a gaping hole underneath.

On hands and knees, he peered into the darkness. Then, wriggling into the hole, he climbed down on to a large concrete step. There he stood for a moment, looking, listening.

The tunnel-like passage was dark, except for the dim glow of light coming from the candle still burning in his chamber.

As he pulled the cloak from beneath his feet and descended another step, he felt a firm hand on his shoulder. He froze. Then he heard comforting words. 'Fear not. It is I.' The voice was strong, self-assured and Gilbert recognised it instantly.

It belonged to the sorcerer Imorex.

Gilbert turned to face the sorcerer. 'You're late,' he said, sullen-faced.

Imorex held a small glass bottle outward. 'These things take time.'

Gilbert took the bottle, ran his fingers down the glass and studied the blue powder inside. 'How much should I – ?'

'The entire bottle,' replied Imorex with a nod.

While Gilbert shoved the bottle in his pocket, Imorex pointed a finger forward and said, 'Your freedom awaits.'

They descended three more steps and made their way along the underground passage.

After walking in a relatively straight line for several minutes, the two men arrived at a green-coloured casket.

Opening it, Gilbert's eyes widened. Although he fully expected the diamond to be inside, he still wasn't prepared for the sheer beauty that was facing back at him. Raising the diamond to his lips, he kissed it.

In that instant, he suddenly understood why a person would kill for this precious jewel and why wars would be fought over it.

If the legends were correct, he could've made an immediate wish, but he was almost afraid to contemplate such a thought with Imorex standing right next to him.

Instead, he passed the diamond over to Imorex, who said nothing as he slipped the jewel into the pocket of his robe.

Then, without so much as a word, the sorcerer set off along the underground passage, back towards the chamber.

Gilbert didn't follow.

He still had *one* more job to do.

CHAPTER FORTY-SEVEN

Gilbert's Betrayal

Shrouded in his black cloak, Gilbert looked menacing; supernatural, even. Under this costume, he felt invisible and somewhat detached from what lay ahead.

This would help, for the moment was now at hand. Standing outside the king's chamber, he knocked quietly twice.

There was no reply. Dropping to his knees, he pushed his ear against the door and listened. He could hear nothing.

As expected, King Jacob was not in his chamber. But what of the queen? Strangely, Queen Belle hadn't been seen for many months.

Rumours, of course, abounded. She was hiding the imminent arrival of the supposed future saviour; she had died and, fearing exposure of this, Zara had concealed her passing.

It hardly matters, Gilbert thought, unlatching the door and sneaking inside. It was time for him to focus on his task.

Removing the hood from his head, he walked further inside, his expression one of sheer amazement. Having never been in this chamber before, he found it overwhelming.

His black boots stood on polished white stone and a roaring fire illuminated the chamber. To his right were bags of gold and on his left were glass cabinets filled with the finest wine.

He felt he had been proved right. King Jacob was watching a crumbling kingdom from the comfort of the richest chamber in the entire palace. To Gilbert, that was unacceptable. Rather than sit idly by and watch this, he would take action.

The fire suddenly crackled, and he jumped. He was stalling. Quickly, he went over to a nearby table on which stood a long-stemmed golden goblet, which he filled to the brim with wine.

Trembling, he lifted the bottle of poison from his pocket and sprinkled the powder into the goblet.

There was now a coat of blue residue lingering on the surface of the wine. He swayed the goblet from side to side, dissolving the deadly powder into the liquid, watching as it vanished.

Turning, he left unobtrusively, only stopping when he had reached the relative safety of the underground once more. Knowing he had accomplished the job, he ran back towards his chamber.

When he came to the first stone step, he could just about see the outline of the sorcerer, standing in the darkness.

'Is it over?' the sorcerer asked.

Gilbert nodded, removing his hood entirely. 'He needs to drink it first.'

Imorex showed the hint of a rare smile. 'He will!'

Gilbert ascended the stairs and climbed back into his chamber. When he had flung the key and the bottle on his bed, he returned to the underground passage once more. Then he followed the sorcerer, who had already located an escape route.

★

Noah, who had been sitting outside Gilbert's chamber door for some time, suddenly noticed Kila storming down the corridor towards him.

'Which part didn't you understand?' Kila called out.

Noah squirmed in his chair. 'Gilbert said it could wait until morning.'

'Well, it can't,' raged Kila, who raised his fist and rapped twice on the door. 'Gilbert, open up, it's Kila!'

The two knights listened, but heard only their own anxious breaths.

Kila turned to Noah, who shrugged and said, 'He hasn't moved from the chamber.' Kila's blue eyes flashed with anger.

'I'm telling the truth.' Noah stood up. 'I spoke to Gilbert. He said that he was feeling unwell and wanted to rest. I've been here ever since. I haven't taken my eyes from his door since the moment he closed it.'

Kila turned and faced the thick door again, desperately trying to hide his rising fear.

CHAPTER FORTY-EIGHT

The Winning Side

King Jacob had retired to his chamber. He lifted an iron poker from beside the hearth and livened the fire. Then he went to the far side of the chamber and, pulling a pair of purple curtains to one side, entered an adjoining room.

He stood still for a moment so that his beautiful wife Belle could sleep peacefully. Finally, sitting down next to her, he took her hand in his.

Queen Belle awoke slowly. 'It's a boy,' she told him. 'Soon, my love, you will have an heir to the throne – the future King of Zara.'

King Jacob gave a warm smile. 'Or the future King of Orchestra, if the prophecies are to be believed.'

Queen Belle was frowning. 'Jacob, you know how I feel about the prophecies.' Her tone was defiant. 'This land will never need a saviour, for there will never be any evil. You're far too good a king to ever let that happen.'

King Jacob forced a worried smile. 'Perhaps.'

'What is it?' Queen Belle shook her head. 'What's wrong?'

'It's Gilbert,' replied King Jacob with a sigh. 'I believe he is betraying me.'

'Gilbert? But he's the leader of the knights. Even Kila speaks highly of him.'

King Jacob nodded sadly.

Queen Belle sat up. 'Well, have you confronted him about it?'

'I don't need to,' replied King Jacob. 'Just the other night, two of my knights followed him through the forest.'

Queen Belle looked questioningly at her husband.

'Oh, I'm afraid he didn't stop there,' King Jacob went on. 'He climbed the bank and entered Darken. My knights rushed back immediately to tell me.'

'Well, could they have been mistaken?' asked Queen Belle.

'He was met by Imorex.'

Queen Belle turned deathly pale.

'No knight of Zara has any business being in Darken,' said King Jacob. 'Especially not now – we're at war.'

'So what will you do?'

'The only thing I can. An act of treason, no matter who you are, can't go unpunished.'

Noticing his wife's anxious eyes, King Jacob drew her attention away from Gilbert and towards their unborn child. 'What shall we call him?'

'I like James,' replied Queen Belle, whose face had already broken into a smile.

King Jacob smiled back. 'Then James Clyde it is.' He laid a solicitous hand on her shoulder. 'Now, I suggest you get some rest. Please don't worry, everything will turn out fine.' Then he walked across the chamber, drew the curtains and entered his own room.

As usual, his servants had his customary drink prepared, but the wine seemed cloudy. *A new vintage*, he presumed, lifting the goblet and bringing it to his lips.

★

Using his shoulder, Kila hurled himself at the door, sending it crashing to the floor. He leapt over the fallen door and ran into the chamber. 'Gilbert!' he shouted, looking around at what appeared to be an empty chamber.

Again, this time more alarmingly, nobody responded.

'Look!' cried Noah, pointing an anxious finger towards the bed, 'the key to the diamond.'

Kila suddenly noticed the disturbed statue and the giant hole beneath it. 'Quick,' he commanded, 'check the diamond's still there!'

Puzzled, Noah lifted the key and slid down into the hole.

Kila stood rooted to the spot, studying his surroundings in disbelief. For the first time, a seed of doubt had entered his mind.

Looking over his shoulder, he stared nervously at a small bottle lying on the bed. It seemed out of place with the décor of the chamber. Tentatively, he walked over. As he reached down for the bottle, he didn't know what to expect.

Screwing the lid open, he stared inside and could just about see the remnants of a blue powder. He placed his nose to the bottle and smelt.

He recognised it.

Poison!

And not just any poison. This powder was one of the few in Orchestra that didn't have an antidote. If the king took even a sip of a drink containing this poison, he would be dead before the goblet had left his lips.

Turning, he sprinted out the chamber door and along the corridor, sensing events had taken a tragic turn. When the king's chamber came into view, he prayed that he wasn't too late.

Without slowing, he charged at the door and it fell through easily. Face down, he could feel dampness beneath him. Blood? It was impossible to tell. In the faint light, the liquid looked black.

As he rose to his feet, a cry of anguish caused him to turn.

The sickening sight that the firelight revealed was one that Kila's nightmares would never allow him to forget.

Queen Belle lay sobbing, her lifeless husband cradled in her arms.

Kila dropped to his knees and, looking up at the oval-shaped ceiling, roared with pain.

★

Gilbert and Imorex arrived at the Orchestra Ocean, where a small wooden boat, occupied by two Volens, lay anchored just beside the bank. The two men climbed into the boat. When they were seated, the Volens began to row.

The three moons of Orchestra lit the night sky and the water glistened in the silvery light. Strangely, an eerie silence had developed around the ocean and the surrounding forest.

Usually at night, dolphins could be seen gliding through the water, but not tonight. The only noise that could be heard was the sound of the oars pushing through the water.

It was as if every single living creature in Zara already knew the terrible news about their king.

Although he should have felt better by now, doubts had surfaced in Gilbert's mind. *Have I done the right thing?*

The two accomplices sat silently in the boat and then finally, when the end of the ocean came into view, Gilbert removed the black hood from his head, revealing his worried face. 'They will surely seek revenge.'

'Let them,' Imorex replied. 'We have two diamonds now. We're only one step away. Besides, any response from Zara would be motivated by hatred and anger. Without a battle plan, they would fight bravely, but die quickly.'

Gilbert still harboured doubts.

The sorcerer smiled coldly. 'Trust me, Gilbert,' he said. 'The Zara you once knew no longer exists. Tonight, they are truly lost. Besides, Abigail has informed me that she will be personally sending an army to attack them. Very soon, we will have all three diamonds.'

A brief silence hung in the air.

'You did well tonight, Gilbert,' Imorex went on. 'You claimed the second diamond and you've also ensured that the son of Jacob will never be a problem.'

Gilbert removed his cloak completely and cast it overboard, watching as the cloth submerged, before finally vanishing from sight into the deep water. He felt clean again. He looked up at the three moons in the starry sky, then smiled and felt better.

The sorcerer was right – he had joined the winning side.

CHAPTER FORTY-NINE

Son of Zara

The council chamber was the largest room in the entire palace, and yet the least decorated.

There were no ornate furnishings or huge chandeliers hanging overhead. Instead, rickety benches and rusty lanterns were positioned around the chamber. There were no windows and only one door, which was usually locked and guarded by two knights.

Tonight, however, the large bronze door was wide open…

'We must attack Darken immediately,' cried Matthew, glancing around the crowded chamber. 'We can't delay any longer.'

Joseph shook his head. 'We must mourn our king first and give him a proper burial.'

All this time, Kila sat motionless on a high chair, his face hidden in his hands.

Joseph walked towards him. 'Kila, you're our leader now. What should we do?'

After a tense moment of silence, Kila got up, ignored everyone and ascended the staircase in search of his queen, who had gone into labour some time earlier.

Halfway up, he bumped into a pair of orchins, both of whom were beaming broad smiles. Bewildered, he stared at them. 'What is it?'

The smaller of the two spoke first. 'He has been born.'

Gilbert and Imorex arrived at Darken Castle and walked quickly towards the queen's throne.

Queen Abigail was staring straight ahead with her lifeless eyes, her image bordering on frightening as her two cats moved around her throne as if they already knew the good news.

Imorex walked over to his throne-like chair, sat down on the purple velvet, removed the hat from his head and ran a tired hand over his white hair. It had been quite a night.

'We have good news, Your Majesty,' Gilbert announced proudly. 'The king is dead and Zara is in complete chaos.' Although he fully expected the queen to be overjoyed, he sensed she was still unimpressed.

'And the diamond?' she grumbled, straight-faced.

Gilbert nodded. 'Got it.'

Queen Abigail glanced at Imorex, who nodded.

'Excellent. We'll finish them off tonight,' said Queen Abigail. 'You've done well, Gilbert. I will see to the downfall of Zara personally.' Lifting the robe from beneath her boots, she climbed confidently to her feet. 'Prepare my army for battle.'

★

In the north wing of the palace, Kila walked quietly into Queen Belle's chamber, where she was sitting up in bed. Her newborn son was wrapped in swaddling clothes and cradled lovingly in her arms.

Grampian, meanwhile, sat beside the bed with a few other orchins who had helped in the delivery.

'Kila,' said Queen Belle, holding her baby upwards, 'I would like you to meet my son, James Clyde.'

Carefully, Kila took the baby in his arms and looked proudly down. 'Hello, James. You are a shining light in these dark days and you are truly a gift to Zara.'

Joseph walked into the chamber and went to Kila. When he saw the child, he allowed himself a little smile.

Kila smiled back at him.

'It's funny, Kila,' said Joseph, peering down at James. He paused and his smile widened. 'This baby is foretold to be the saviour of Orchestra, but his birth has *already* saved this land.'

Kila looked at Joseph, then down at James. He knew exactly what Joseph meant: just by being born, James Clyde had given a perpetual hope and a will to live to so many people of Zara.

True, they had lost a king, but they had gained a son.

CHAPTER FIFTY

Queen Abigail Attacks Zara

Queen Abigail of Darken got into her carriage, followed closely by Imorex, who signalled the Volen in front to leave.

At once, the Volen nodded and cracked the reins, sending the four strong horses galloping towards Zara.

Gilbert wasn't travelling with them. The sorcerer Imorex feared the sight of him in Zara might have the unwelcome effect of rallying their troops.

'You've played your part, my friend,' Imorex had told Gilbert earlier in the castle. *'Darken will forever be indebted to your contribution. Rest tonight. We will finish this.'*

Now, sitting inside the carriage, a diamond cradled in his hands, Imorex didn't regret his decision. Gilbert wasn't needed.

The army assembled was more than sufficient – Volens were already on large boats, sailing across the ocean and heavily armed Dakotas had long since left, flying in healthy numbers towards Zara.

Besides, his visions tonight, apart from *one*, had been very encouraging. He fully expected Zara to fall.

Feeling relaxed, the Queen of Darken sat comfortably on her soft velvet seat and sensed victory was near. She looked at Imorex beside her. 'You're sure they've found the last diamond?'

Imorex nodded. 'Certain. We are one step away.'

The queen smiled as she gazed down at the diamond nestled in the sorcerer's hands.

Imorex noticed her roving eye and said, 'Tonight, Abigail, you will be the most powerful person in Orchestra.'

Queen Abigail extended an eager hand towards the diamond but, unexpectedly, Imorex clenched his fist closed.

When Queen Abigail looked up, she thought the sorcerer seemed tense. 'What's the matter?' she asked.

Imorex squirmed in his seat. 'Abigail, before you make your wish, I have something to tell you.' He raised his white eyebrows. 'I'm afraid this night didn't go quite as well as I had first hoped.'

Imorex now had the queen's undivided attention.

'What do you mean?' she snapped, nodding at the diamond. 'We have the diamond and you said it yourself, Zara will be defeated tonight.' Her voice was angry now. 'I mean you assured me of that –'

Imorex held a hand aloft. 'Zara will almost certainly fall tonight,' he told her. 'But I need to draw your attention to something before you make your next wish.'

'Go on.'

Imorex scratched his head before continuing. 'Unless my visions have been wrong, and they rarely are, then…' He took a deep breath. 'Abigail, how can I tell you this?'

Queen Abigail had grown impatient. 'Just tell me, Imorex,' she told him. 'I'm looking at the second diamond of Orchestra in your hands. Now, tell me, on this wonderful night, what could possibly be wrong?'

Imorex looked her dead in the eye. 'The saviour has been born.'

The words seemed to linger in the air for a moment.

The queen shut her eyes, as if in quiet resignation, and she couldn't help thinking that centuries-old prophecies were almost mocking her attempts to change the course of destiny. She grabbed the precious diamond out of Imorex's hand.

'Choose wisely, Abigail,' Imorex warned her. 'This gift must be useful. Remember, we have no guarantee of obtaining the last diamond tonight.'

Queen Abigail brought the powerful and legendary diamond towards her face. 'This child,' she said slowly, 'will one day wish he had never been born.'

With the glint of the diamond reflecting in her eyes, Queen Abigail of Darken made her wish. For a brief moment, the carriage lit up. When the queen reopened her eyes, she smiled deviously.

★

Inside the Zaran palace, mother and child slept peacefully, unaware of the danger approaching from the forest.

The chamber was now empty and only a dozen or so knights, led by the commanding presence of their leader, Kila, stood outside the door, keeping a close watch.

All of a sudden, the war trumpet sounded and Joseph shot Kila a nervous look. 'They're coming, Kila,' he said. 'We have to act now.'

Kila nodded. 'Go and find Grampian.'

Joseph nodded back. 'What will you do?'

'I'll stay here and watch over them. Now go!'

'I won't be long,' cried Joseph, sprinting down the corridor.

Kila entered the queen's chamber and made his way towards the nearest window.

Queen Belle sat up. 'That was the war trumpet, wasn't it?'

Kila turned to look at her. 'Yes, Your Majesty.'

'We're under attack, aren't we?'

Kila closed his eyes and nodded.

'She's coming for him, isn't she?'

Kila shrugged. 'If she's aware he has been born, then yes she's probably here for him. But I'd be surprised if she did know. It's more likely she's here for the diamond.'

Just then, a series of violent screams erupted; Kila ran over to the window, parted the red curtains and peered sadly down at the courtyard, where he saw his knights being slaughtered in large numbers.

His first instinct was to leave and help his men, but he knew his main priority was the safety of his queen and her newborn son.

Kila was still arguing with himself about what he should do next when Grampian came quietly into the chamber. 'Grampian, do you know how to get them to safety?'

'Leave it to me, Kila,' said Grampian with a confident nod. 'I know where they should go.'

At that moment, a knight of Zara charged into the chamber, his arm dripping with blood.

'Kila,' the man shouted, 'we are losing too many men. We're being destroyed. We need you down there.'

Kila looked at Grampian, who nodded reassuringly and said, 'I'll get them to safety. You go help your men.'

As he ran towards the door, Kila knew something still bothered him. He stopped, turned around and looked at the knight of Zara, who had just rushed into the chamber moments earlier.

'Knight, what is your name?' said Kila.

Nursing his arm, the knight replied, 'Wilmore.'

Kila smiled. 'Wilmore, I want you to go with Belle and James. I want you to protect them.'

'With my life, master,' said Wilmore staunchly.

'I thought you'd say that,' said Kila. Then he turned, walked from the chamber and began to switch his attention towards the battle awaiting him outside. He knew it was probably too late for him to change the outcome, but he could always try. *I will try!*

As he went down the grand staircase, he suddenly sensed a presence nearby, as if somebody was watching him.

Slowing down and listening intently, he glanced over his shoulder a couple of times and let his eyes explore the palace.

He saw nothing, and yet he felt certain he wasn't alone. He paced down the stairs, conscious he was being watched.

Suddenly, footsteps appeared from nowhere. Before he had a chance to turn, he felt his head snap backwards, while a sharp cord of wire wrapped around his throat from behind.

Instantly, his feet were lifted off the stairs and he felt his lungs straining for air.

Out of the corner of his eye, he could see the large hand of a Volen clasping the wire. As he felt the delicate skin of his throat begin to bleed, he heard a venomous voice speak, just behind his left ear.

'The great Kila.'

Then the cord tightened. Kila threw a backward kick in an attempt to free himself, but it had little effect.

'I'll make this very simple,' said the Volen in his usual deep tone. 'Tell me *where* the diamond is and I will kill you quickly.'

Kila made no attempt to speak.

The Volen's fury grew. He heaved the wire fiercely back and the sinews of Kila's neck bulged through his beard. His face contorted into a painful grimace.

'WHERE'S THE DIAMOND?'

Fighting for his life, Kila rammed the Volen against the wall, crushing him, but the large animal hung on to the cord and pulled it back even more.

Choking, Kila suddenly eyed a neglected bottle of wine lying on one of the steps. It was partially broken and a potential weapon.

Using his strength, he swayed towards the bottle and reached it with his second attempt. Holding the bottle by the neck, he swung it over his shoulder, connecting cleanly with the Volen's head. The bottle broke in half, spraying the marble walls.

Kila fully expected the Volen to collapse next, but the brute was still standing behind him, pulling the cord of wire back with violent trusts.

Kila's bloodshot eyes fell on the remaining steps of the staircase. Although the fall would probably kill them both, he knew that he had run out of options.

He hurled himself down, the Volen clinging on tightly as they both rolled down the stairs with crushing force, their heads smashing against the hard marble along the way in turn.

Landing at the bottom, Kila ignored the stars that had entered his vision and scrambled for his belt. Lifting the first weapon his hand met, he plunged the dagger into the Volen's neck.

As it happened, the Volen was already dead from the fall.

Breathless, Kila gave himself a second before lifting his battered body from the floor. Coughing blood, he wrapped a hand across his throat.

After taking a deep, but uncomfortable breath, he hunched over and placed his hands on his knees.

★

Inside the king's chamber, Queen Belle was worried about Wilmore, who had almost collapsed from his loss of blood and was now sitting on the bed resting.

Queen Belle noticed that the cut was deep and almost travelled the entire length of Wilmore's lower left arm.

Concerned, she lifted a cloth from her bedside locker and, using it as a dressing, wrapped it a couple of times around the wound.

'Thank you,' muttered Wilmore.

Queen Belle turned to Grampian. 'Can you do something about this bleeding?'

'I'm afraid we don't have time, Your Majesty,' Grampian told her.

Wilmore waved the suggestion off. 'I'll be fine,' he declared. 'Besides, we have to keep moving. We can't hold them for much longer.'

★

At the foot of the grand staircase, blood-soaked knights began to gather around Kila, who had recovered slightly.

Joseph looked at Kila clutching his throat. 'Are you alright?'

Kila nodded, then drew his sword and walked stubbornly

towards the palace doors. It seemed odd to him that the noise outside had died. Still, he continued walking.

'I wouldn't go out there,' said Joseph, holding out a restraining hand and stopping Kila in his tracks.

Kila's eyes narrowed. 'Why not?'

Joseph took a deep breath, as if to compose himself for what he had to say next. '*She* is here and Imorex is with her.'

Kila shrugged. 'All the more reason to walk out the front door!'

'Wait,' cried Joseph.

Glancing at the small number of knights beside Joseph, Kila commanded, 'Gather the rest of the knights. We'll charge them down.'

'Just wait,' Joseph repeated.

Kila turned, and, sword in hand, walked belligerently towards the doors once more.

Joseph shouted after him, 'They're *all* dead.'

Kila turned, certain he'd heard wrong. 'What?'

When Joseph spoke, his voice trembled. 'The knights are all dead, Kila.' He pointed to the small gathering of knights behind him. 'We're all that's left. We've been wiped out.'

By the time the words had sunk in, Kila had already started to feel physically sick. *All the knights are dead? All my friends?*

Kila knew some of these knights had been very young. He suddenly hated himself. These men were his responsibility, just as his king had been before them.

The terrible silence in the chamber lasted a while before Joseph took two steps forward. 'So, what should we do?'

Kila lifted his sword and his determined eyes seemed to focus upon it. Rubbing the blade, he switched his attention to a life-sized mirror and his own reflection.

Blood was rolling down his brow like perspiration. He smiled, seeming to take great pleasure in his disfigured appearance. He turned to look at Joseph. '*We fight!*'

CHAPTER FIFTY-ONE

James Sent to Earth

Stepping over mutilated bodies, Queen Abigail and the sorcerer Imorex paced through the partially broken gates of the palace.

The air was eerily silent, apart from the occasional groan of pain or plea for help, which went unheard.

The battle was over. Darken had won, but Queen Abigail's expression was still sour. The hard work, she knew, began now.

Despite the numerous bodies, it didn't take long for them to reach the palace doors. Walking quickly inside, they looked around, scanning their surroundings purposefully.

★

Inside the royal chamber, Grampian knew he had to hurry. Wasting no time, he rushed over to a silver casket that was positioned at the far side of the chamber.

Wilmore looked on in astonishment. 'What are you doing?' he cried. 'We've to leave right away.'

'The diamond!' said Grampian, handing Wilmore a gold key. 'Do hurry.'

When Wilmore opened the casket, the sight of the diamond sent a shiver down his spine. Although he had heard whispers that magical diamonds had been found, a part of him had remained incredulous.

As a man of logic, he didn't need anyone to tell him that the diamond now nestled in his hands wasn't supposed to exist, and yet, against all the odds, it did. This made him smile.

After placing the diamond safely in the bag hanging over his shoulder, he looked back at Grampian for the next move.

'Let's get going,' said Grampian, turning to the others. 'They're already in the palace.'

'I'm not going,' said Queen Belle, looking at Grampian, whose shocked face conveyed a thousand words.

'What do you mean you're not going?' he replied in horror. 'You're the queen – you must leave.'

Queen Belle was shaking her head. '*James* needs to leave,' she told him. 'I must stay. I won't abandon my people when they need me the most.' Then she walked over to Wilmore. 'Please look after him, Wilmore. Treat him kindly and bring him back one day to fulfil his destiny.'

Wilmore gave a reassuring nod. 'I will,' he said.

Queen Belle smiled at him. 'From this day forth, I want you to look upon yourself as a Clyde.'

Wilmore smiled proudly back.

Pushing the bed to one side, Grampian opened a trapdoor and he and Wilmore, who was carrying James in his arms, descended into it.

Queen Belle, tearful and emotional, kissed her son one last time. Then she closed the trapdoor, slid the bed back to normal and waited.

★

Moments earlier, Queen Abigail and Imorex had strode methodically towards the grand staircase of the palace, where they had been met by 12 intimidating men, all standing shoulder width apart, blocking their progress.

Now, the 12 knights, led by the imposing figure of Kila, stared at the queen with looks of disgust and scorn.

Queen Abigail smiled coldly. 'I do not wish you any harm,' she said. 'Tell me where the diamond is and I'll spare your lives.'

Kila looked at Imorex, then at Queen Abigail. 'You should both turn back now.' He nodded at the dead Volen whose smashed body lay on the floor. 'Unless, of course, you want to end up like your friend over there.'

Queen Abigail gave a mirthless laugh. 'And would you be the knight called Kila?'

Kila didn't react.

Queen Abigail breathed deeply. 'A pleasure to finally meet you,' she said. 'Your reputation precedes you.' Then, as easily as a magician splitting a deck of cards, she swung her hands in opposite directions and the knights parted.

Immobilised, the knights could only watch as Queen Abigail and Imorex strolled past them up the stairs.

When they had reached the top, the two accomplices gazed around at the different chambers, deciding which one to check.

A moment later, they made their move.

★

Deep beneath the palace, Wilmore held James close and ran as fast as he had ever run in his entire life through the dark underground passage. Breathless, he reluctantly stopped and listened.

Through the floorboards overhead, the sounds of heavy footsteps could be heard. He knew it would only be a matter of time before the Volens picked up on his trail.

Glancing down at the satchel hanging across his upper body, he noticed the green shine of the diamond, while in his arms he carried the saviour of the world.

It was then that he grasped the enormity of his situation. 'Grampian,' he whispered, 'where are you?'

'Right here,' said a voice, emerging from the darkness.

'Where'd you go?' said Wilmore, sounding frantic. 'And how did you get here so fast?'

'Orchins,' said Grampian, 'have their ways.'

'We'll be found here,' said Wilmore, listening to the sound of Volen humming just above his head.

'That's why you and James are leaving this instant,' replied Grampian, digging into the small bag around his shoulder. After a lengthy search, he lifted out a long, silver, cylindrical shaped object and held it outwards.

Wilmore frowned and said, 'What's that?'

'It's a transporter,' said Grampian with pride. 'It will transport you to the other world, just by pressing this red button at the top.' He lifted a finger towards the transporter, then stopped and looked at Wilmore. 'I'd stand back if I were you.'

As Wilmore took a few paces back, Grampian pushed the button at the top of the transporter and a single wooden door appeared.

Wilmore frowned, unable to believe it. The wooden door looked normal, but for one exception: at the very top was a handle with the word: ORCHESTRA.

'The door you see before you happens to be a gateway to another world.' Grampian pointed to the handle high up on the door as he was much too small to reach.

Wilmore reached upwards with his uninjured hand and turned the handle. The word *ORCHESTRA* changed to *EARTH*.

Opening the door, Wilmore found himself staring into a dark abyss. He looked at Grampian once more. 'How will I bring James back?'

Grampian nodded. 'We will call him and find a way.'

'Let me guess – orchins have their ways,' said Wilmore, breaking into a smile.

Grampian smiled back. 'Exactly!' From under his hat, he lifted a crumbled note and slipped it inside Wilmore's satchel. 'Now, before you go, please listen to me very carefully.'

'What was that?' said Wilmore.

'It's an address of where you will live. You will find safety there and enough money to provide for you and James for a very long time.'

'Money?'

Grampian smiled. 'You'll soon understand.'

Taking a deep breath, Wilmore stared into the blackness of the doorway once more.

Grampian took two steps forward. Standing side by side, they both peered into the vast chasm of dark space.

'Remember, Wilmore,' said Grampian passionately, 'James Clyde *must* live.'

As Wilmore stared into the abyss, the baby in his arms gave a faint cry. He looked down and James Clyde peered back, wide-eyed and oblivious to his importance. The infant's innocent eyes locked upon Wilmore's fretful ones.

He nodded at Grampian before jumping feet-first into the unknown.

Grampian looked into the empty darkness.

They were gone.

He smiled, pressed the top of the transporter and watched as the door incinerated with a puff of smoke.

★

Queen Abigail and the sorcerer Imorex had now reached King Jacob's chamber. They scanned the area, their eyes trying to locate even the faintest glow of emerald green.

Nothing.

Out of the corner of her eye, Queen Abigail spotted a wooden crib lying beside the bed. 'It's true, then?'

'You're too late, Abigail,' said Queen Belle, emerging from the shadows. 'He *has* been born, and he is safe.'

'Safe is a point of view,' replied Queen Abigail. 'Once I have the last diamond of Orchestra, I will be more powerful than anyone in this land.' She moved closer. 'I know it's here and I want it.'

'The diamond is safe now,' Queen Belle told her. 'It's far away from Orchestra and far away from you.'

'And your son?'

There was no answer.

Queen Abigail paced forward. 'You're trying to hide him, aren't you? Well, you needn't bother. I will find him. Let's not draw it out any longer than necessary. Tell me where he went!'

Queen Belle made no effort to respond.

Queen Abigail lifted her right hand and suddenly Queen Belle was no longer standing; instead, she was 20 feet in the air.

'Come now,' said the Queen of Darken. 'Bring him to me.' She looked around the chamber. 'Let me meet the saviour.'

'No!'

'If you defy me, I will make you suffer greatly – more than you could ever care to imagine. Now bring him to me.'

'No!'

'BRING HIM TO ME!'

'I will never tell you anything.'

Queen Abigail squeezed her fingertips together. Queen Belle, who suddenly felt her throat beginning to tighten, fought for breath.

'Then there won't be any need for you, will there?' Queen Abigail said with a snigger, swinging her right hand to the side.

Like a rag doll, Queen Belle was tossed around the chamber, her skull cracking against the walls with terrible force.

On and on it went, from one corner of the chamber to the other, her long blonde hair hiding her shattered face.

The sight of blood smearing the walls made Queen Abigail stop. She lowered her hand and Queen Belle fell to the floor, barely conscious.

'Bring her back to Darken,' Queen Abigail commanded to a Volen, who had just entered the chamber after hearing the commotion, 'and search for the diamond. She might've been lying.'

'Yes, Your Majesty,' said the Volen.

'Oh and by the way,' added Queen Abigail, 'kill the 12 men at the bottom of the stairs.'

The Volen nodded. 'As you wish.' Then he left.

Moments later, Queen Abigail and Imorex walked from the chamber.

Imorex turned to Queen Abigail. 'All is not lost,' he told her. 'I know where the child has gone. Find the child and we will find the diamond.'

'Your Majesty,' interrupted a Volen, reappearing again.

Queen Abigail groaned. 'What is it now?'

'Um, Your Majesty. I think you'd better –'

The queen turned, angry. 'Is there a problem?'

The Volen looked confused. 'Well, yes, Your Majesty,' he said. 'There are *no* men at the bottom of the stairs.'

CHAPTER FIFTY-TWO

Gilbert Approaches

James had listened attentively to the whole story and, as expected, some parts had been hard to hear. However, he had a lot of questions that needed answering.

'So Wilmore wasn't my grandfather?'

Joseph shook his head. 'No, but he looked upon you as his grandson.'

'When will they attack us again?' said James with a frown.

Nathan sighed. 'Nobody knows.'

Joseph smiled when he saw how worried James looked. 'All will be well,' he assured him. 'Let's not worry.' Rising, he patted James on the arm. 'Now then, I think it's about time we had something to eat, don't you?'

James nodded, but he was still trying to fully grasp the story he had just heard. He wasn't sure how he felt.

After a moment, he got up, left the courtyard and followed the knights into the palace.

★

In Darken, Queen Abigail stood up from her throne, looking like a woman on the verge of completing an 11 year mission. 'Kill the boy and search the palace for the diamond,' she instructed Gilbert in a loud voice. 'They have it somewhere. Find it!'

'Yes, Your Majesty,' replied Gilbert, and he bowed. He walked from the hall, climbed several flights of stairs and slipped into a very elegant-looking chamber of the castle.

Without breaking his stride, he pushed through a pair of dark red curtains separating the chamber from the outside balcony. Peering downwards, he saw, to his obvious delight, that the entire courtyard was crowded with Volens.

In the sky, meanwhile, Dakotas flew menacingly around, their claws bearing swords and spears. The numbers had increased exponentially since he had last checked.

'Kill the boy and find the diamond!' he commanded strongly. 'Do not fail me.'

With frightening speed, the Volens dashed through the Darken forest and down the bank, only stopping when they had reached the large boats that were anchored beside the Zaran forest.

One of the Volens cut the anchor with a knife and more of the animals streamed into the vessel.

When it was full, they were the first to set sail.

★

Inside the Zaran palace, everybody had just sat down to an orchin-prepared meal, which smelt good and tasted even better.

'Why are there only 12 of you left?' said Ben, sipping water.

'We're the only survivors of the war,' replied Joseph, spreading butter on his bread.

Ben gasped. 'The only survivors? How many knights were there?'

'Just over five hundred,' said Joseph. 'The rest of the knights were either captured or killed. Those captured were taken as prisoners and are now jailed in Darken.'

Kila looked at Ben. 'We simply don't have the power to free them. They wait in the dungeons at Darken, hoping and praying that one day they'll be freed.' He looked across the table at James, who had reddened slightly.

Ben extended a hand and helped himself to the juicy red grapes that were lying in glass bowls around the table. After popping one in his mouth, he asked a question that had been puzzling him for some time. 'Why has Abigail not come back here and captured you?'

'We're no threat to her,' explained Matthew. 'She also knew the last diamond of Orchestra wasn't here.'

'She hasn't set foot here in 11 years,' remarked David.

James looked at him. 'Why not?'

'Because of you,' said Noah.

'Me? But I haven't been here.'

Noah drank from his goblet, then continued. 'That doesn't matter. She's scared of the prophecies of this land. She won't return while the threat of James Clyde looms large over Orchestra.'

'She's really that scared of me?'

'Yes,' said Gabriel. 'Your name signifies hope to the people and that scares her.'

Kila was nodding. 'You see, James, she wants the power of the three diamonds before she would even think about facing the great James Clyde, her prophesied conqueror.' He broke a loaf of bread in two and started chewing on one half. 'But we have the last diamond, so that's not going to happen.'

★

At the verge of the Zaran forest, the remaining Volens climbed into the boats, pulled the anchors on board and set sail across the Orchestra Ocean.

The boat in which Gilbert stood was the largest of the fleet – seven luxurious cabins on deck and a holding area for weapons.

Gilbert looked very authoritative, like a teacher overseeing a class excursion, but being in charge came with a heavy price. If they returned without the diamond, it was his fault. If they were defeated, he took the blame.

But he enjoyed the responsibility and knew he owed everything to his queen. She had set him free. 11 years ago, Queen Abigail had given him his chance.

'I know it might pain you,' the queen had told him, 'but you will be doing Orchestra a great service. Your betrayal will *free* her.' The words had struck a cord with him. *I will be freeing my land. I will be the saviour.*

Cementing his place in history was also important. As a knight, he was just another number; a member of an organisation. It was hardly the life he had envisaged for himself.

In the end, it was Queen Abigail's vision that had bribed him. It was a chance of a new life; a better existence than the mundane duties of a knight. Now he had power and responsibility, something which he would never have had in Zara.

A small swell awoke him from his daydream. He leaned his arms on the side of the boat, watching the powerful vessel cutting through the ocean, spraying water up on to his face. He found himself fantasising about the last diamond once more.

Like everyone in Orchestra, he was mystified by the diamonds.

Where had they come from? Who had made them? Why were they so powerful?

He had asked himself these questions on countless occasions, but he simply didn't have the answers. But he did know this: he wanted some of the diamonds' power.

Looking out across the ocean and watching boats passing his own, it suddenly struck him that they were going about this ambush the wrong way.

'Stop the boats!' he roared, racing up the deck, waving his hands in the air like the conductor of a choir. 'We're going on foot from here.'

'Why?' said a Volen, confused.

'We can't be seen,' replied Gilbert. 'We have to take them by surprise. Bring the boats to land now!'

The Volen sulked. 'If you insist, Sir.'

They unfurled the sails and brought the boats to land, anchoring them some distance from the palace.

When the boat was stationed, Gilbert jumped from the vessel, ran a hand over his oiled hair and stared into the forest.

★

Inside the Zaran palace, James and Ben, the only two eating all the food, stopped suddenly when Mary came walking into the dining chamber, looking fully rested and ready for a meal.

Kila laughed loudly. 'Ah, Mary, it's good to see you've finally decided to join us. You slept well, I hope?'

Mary yawned, patting her open mouth. 'I slept all night and I had the most wonderful dream.'

'You can sit here,' said Kila, pulling out a chair next to James. 'I hope you like vegetable soup.'

Mary didn't even have to think about it. 'Oh yes,' she said, 'Wilmore used to make it for us all the time.'

'Well, I hope my cooking is just as good,' replied Kila.

Mary frowned hard. She didn't mean any offence: Kila just didn't seem or look the cooking type.

Kila knew he had no culinary skills, so he winked at James and Ben, who both laughed.

★

Looking through tree branches, Gilbert focused his gaze on the giant white gates ahead. He smiled to himself. It felt like he had never been away. Then he turned and commanded, 'Bring the slave with you, but the rest of you stay here.' He straightened his tie and began to walk.

★

As usual, a couple of knights were keeping watch from the balcony. Today, it was Lance and Joel's turn.

Lance stood still, looking through a spyglass. Suddenly he let it drop, the glass shattering on the stone ground.

Far off, he could see a dark figure approaching the gates. Knowing immediately who it was, he looked nervously across at Joel, who looked just as nervously back.

★

Mary slurped the last drop of soup from her spoon and, after wiping her mouth with a napkin, said, 'That was delicious!'

'Why thank you, Mary,' said Kila. 'I have to confess though, I didn't actually cook it.'

Footsteps suddenly sounded on the marble floor, and out of the corner of his eye, Kila could see Ethan approaching the table, his strides urgent.

'Kila, I need a word.'

Sensing something was wrong, Kila got to his feet and brought Ethan to the far side of the chamber. 'What is it?'

Ethan looked at Kila gravely. 'It's Gilbert!'

For a moment, Kila felt the world around him stand still. This name, synonymous with betrayal, hadn't been mentioned by a knight in his presence for the last 11 years. 'What about Gilbert?'

Ethan frowned. 'He's outside the palace gates.'

Kila raised his eyebrows. 'Is he alone?'

'Yes, alone, but he's asked to speak to you privately.'

Kila looked at the dining table and then back at Ethan. 'Listen to me very carefully. Go back to the table, eat some food and don't tell James that Gilbert is here. Pretend that nothing is wrong.' He pulled Ethan closer. 'Do you understand me?'

Ethan nodded, then walked over to the table, asking a question when he arrived. 'Children, have you ever heard me sing before?'

Eric laughed. 'Believe me, children, you don't want to.'

'Nonsense,' exclaimed Ethan, waving the comment off as he burst into a rendition of his favourite song. The horrendous singing was only interrupted when Grampian came striding into the dining chamber, his mere presence gaining instant attention.

'Mary, Ben,' he said softly. 'I need to speak to you both, please.'

'What about?' asked Ben when he had finished eating a crust of bread. 'Ethan was just about to sing –'

Grampian seemed uncharacteristically tense. 'Follow me, please, and you'll get that answer.'

Without another word, Ben and Mary followed Grampian as he left through a side door that led into a long, dark corridor.

★

Outside, Kila walked briskly towards the gates, only to be stopped suddenly when Lance and Joel approached him, their faces pale.

'It's a trap, Kila,' said Lance. 'He's not here alone.'

'He just wants the boy,' added Joel.

'If that's the case, then he has wasted a journey,' replied Kila in a determined tone of voice. 'But I have to see what he wants. Now open the gates.'

A moment later, as commanded, the white gates swung open and Kila walked through.

Far off in the distance, the dark figure of Gilbert stood alone. Kila couldn't believe how little Gilbert's appearance had changed; the receding hair had become no thinner, the moustache and dark eyes were the same. The only difference of note were his black clothes.

Kila decided a 20 yard distance was close enough. Breaking the silence, he asked the most obvious question. 'Why have you come here?' He took a step forward. 'You're not welcome.'

Gilbert flashed a smile. 'It's good to see you again, my old friend.'

CHAPTER FIFTY-THREE

Join Us

Kila felt his limbs weaken. 'I ought to kill you right now. You betrayed Zara, your king and your very soul.' He frowned. 'And for what?'

Gilbert gave a brief smirk. 'For all the power in Orchestra,' he declared. 'The tide is turning. Soon Abigail will have power over the land and you will have nothing but memories.' He edged closer. 'Join us, Kila. It's not too late. Join us, old friend, and you could have a big say in the new regime.'

Kila heaved a sigh. 'You stand for everything I hate. My loyalty and allegiance will always be with Zara and James Clyde.'

Gilbert took a short breath. 'I fear you place too much faith in that boy.'

Kila paced forward and looked sadly at Gilbert. Then, he asked a question that he had pondered and agonised over for almost 12 years. 'How could you betray us like that?'

Gilbert's face showed no emotion. 'The reason was straightforward, Kila,' he said. 'I knew the power of the land was changing. I saw a crumbling kingdom and I took necessary action. Darken offered me power.' He sighed. 'Zara offered me nothing but their sickening beliefs in a so-called saviour who might one day arrive and make this world a better place. The prophecies might have blinded some people, but not me.'

'You went against everything the knights of Zara ever stood

for.' Kila shook his head. 'If you had concerns, you should've spoken to me.'

Gilbert turned away.

Kila thought he detected sadness in Gilbert's demeanour, bringing him back to a time when they were like brothers and when they had understood each other completely. 'You were idolised in Zara.'

Gilbert held up a hand. 'That's quite enough,' he said flatly. 'I'm not here to talk about the past.'

'Then why are you here?'

'Come now, Kila. We both knew this day would arrive, but because I respect you, I'll keep it very simple. Hand over the boy and the diamond and I'll let you and your knights go free.'

Kila was already shaking his head.

Gilbert sighed. 'Then sadly, Kila, you leave me with no other alternative.' Then, looking around at the Zaran forest, the man in black nodded.

- CHAPTER FIFTY-FOUR -

Last Diamond of Orchestra

A Volen appeared from the forest with a prisoner, a knife held across the woman's throat in case she tried to escape.

'Behold your queen,' shouted Gilbert.

'Your Majesty,' cried Kila, stunned.

Queen Belle struggled to get free. 'Don't give them James,' she cried.

'If you make another sudden move.' The Volen rubbed his blade across her throat. 'I will cut you from ear to ear.'

Gilbert exploded with anger. 'HAND OVER THE BOY AND THE DIAMOND OR YOUR QUEEN IS DEAD!'

Still trying to grasp the situation, Kila said, 'I need to speak with the rest of the knights. I don't know where the boy is. He's in hiding and the orchins have the diamond.'

'You're lying, Kila,' replied Gilbert, arching his eyebrows. 'I know you too well. Now, why would you do that? You're playing with your queen's life. With just a click of my fingers I could have her killed before your eyes.'

Kila strode forward. 'Understand this, Gilbert – you're not getting the boy. As I've already said, he is far from here.'

'Is that so?' Gilbert looked far from convinced.

Kila nodded. 'Do you really think I would just leave him here?'

Gilbert shook his head. 'Kila, I have an army ready to tear this place apart looking for him. Get me the diamond and I might persuade them not to.'

'Give me the queen first,' demanded Kila stubbornly.

'You're in no position to make demands. This happens on my terms.' Gilbert nodded at the Volen, who lifted his knife and ran it along Queen Belle's neck, cutting off a lock of blonde hair.

The Volen then held his knife aloft, displaying the lock of hair like a symbol of intent.

Gilbert now vented a fury unlike any Kila had ever witnessed before. 'THE DIAMOND OR YOUR QUEEN'S LIFE!'

Kila stared into Gilbert's dark eyes. 'I'll get the diamond,' he said after a moment. 'Just don't hurt her.'

'Don't give me any reason to.' Gilbert stepped forward and his smile widened under his black moustache. 'You have three minutes!'

★

Inside the palace, Ben and Mary followed Grampian up a flight of stairs, but instead of stopping there, they climbed two more flights until they found themselves in a very small, narrow corridor. It was dimly lit by miniature chandeliers and furnished with beautifully textured red carpet that felt like wool underneath their shoes.

'Where are you taking us?' pressed Mary, glancing around.

'Here,' said Grampian, pointing to a very small chamber door which was big enough for Mary to walk through as she was slightly shorter than Grampian, but Ben knew he had a problem.

'I won't be able to fit in there,' he said.

'You will if you stoop down,' replied Grampian.

Doing as suggested, Ben followed Mary into the chamber.

There was no doubt about it – this was definitely orchin territory. The small upholstered furniture, the tiny garments and the beautifully made musical instruments all gave a clear indication that this chamber belonged to an orchin.

Mary pulled up a wooden chair and sat on it, feeling ready for whatever lay ahead. To pass the time, she looked at Ben, who cracked his head painfully on the ceiling as he moved around.

Mary just couldn't stop herself from laughing. *How wonderful it is to be small*, she reflected, watching Ben massaging his temples.

Having learnt his lesson, Ben lowered on to his knees and crawled over to Mary, frowning at her as he sat down.

Meanwhile, Grampian had already moved towards a cabinet at the far side of the chamber. Opening it, the chamber was suddenly illuminated with jets of blinding green light.

Taking the diamond with him, he walked carefully back towards the children, keeping his eyes on the floor in case he tripped. 'What if I told you that you could have anything you ever wanted? I mean, anything in the entire world?'

'Do you mean we can – ?' Ben pointed to the magnificent diamond before his eyes.

Grampian nodded, then held the diamond outward, almost teasing the children to take it.

Ben, open-mouthed, took the diamond and held it in both hands. After a moment, he closed his eyes and, without speaking, made his wish.

Instantly, the now familiar beams of light flickered around the little chamber. When the lights subsided, Ben re-opened his eyes and smiled at Mary. Then, reaching over, he handed her the diamond.

Mary looked at the diamond in her hand and paused a moment, thinking deeply. Finally, she shut her eyes and appeared to mutter a few words, which, despite trying desperately hard, Ben just couldn't hear.

After a moment, the great light vanished from the chamber and Mary passed the diamond back to Grampian.

'I hope,' said Grampian, 'that you have chosen wisely, for you will need these gifts more than you could ever imagine.' He looked at the children, who nodded and smiled.

Grampian smiled warmly back. 'Now, back to James,' he said,

waving them out. Standing up quickly, Ben thumped his head against the ceiling once more, causing Mary to laugh loudly into her hands.

Ben looked at her sternly and caressed his head as they walked out the door and back along the corridor.

When they entered the dining chamber, they returned to their chairs beside James. A deep yearning to explore their gifts came over them, but they knew that this wasn't the right time or place.

Unable to contain herself, Mary brought her hands to her eyes, studying them closely. To her, they appeared exactly the same.

'What was that all about?' asked James, looking over at Ben and Mary, who smiled back knowingly.

Unexpectedly, Kila burst through the palace doors and into the dining chamber, where word had already spread between the knights that he had been talking to Gilbert.

James turned. By Kila's pale expression, he knew that something was terribly wrong. 'What is it?' he said, peering up.

Kila remained silent as he walked past the table and gathered the 11 knights around him. 'They want the diamond,' he said. 'Go find Grampian.'

Gabriel, who looked shocked by the sudden surrender, said, 'Surely you're not thinking of giving it to them?'

Matthew nodded. 'This cannot be the way.'

Kila frowned, bringing Gabriel quietly to one side. 'I have no choice,' he said. 'They have our queen.'

Gabriel's jaw dropped. 'Queen Belle is alive?'

Kila gave a quick nod. 'I saw her with my own eyes. They'll kill her if we don't give up the diamond.'

Gabriel didn't seem as certain. 'Killing his king was one thing, but would he harm a woman?' He grabbed Kila by the arm. 'Could he have been bluffing?'

'I believed him!' said Kila. 'Besides, we can't take that chance. We will have our queen back and that is all that matters.' He nodded. 'We've James now. That makes the diamond less important than it once was.'

'He's right,' said Noah, listening in.

Kila wiped away beads of sweat forming on his brow. 'We have to do what is right for the kingdom. To lose our queen once was bad enough, but to lose her again would be unforgivable.'

'It's the only thing we can do,' agreed Joseph. The words had barely left Joseph's mouth when Grampian came walking into the chamber, a diamond of Orchestra in his hand. With his customary kind look, he held the diamond towards Kila, who now looked a broken man, tortured by his decision.

'Your heart is kind, Kila,' said Grampian. 'You must follow it. What is it telling you?'

Kila paused, then looked across at James, who was looking straight back at him with worried eyes. 'It's telling me that nothing, not even the diamond, is more important than James Clyde now.'

With a smile, Grampian passed Kila the diamond.

Kila's eyes were filled with sadness. 'I never thought that this day would arrive,' he said, turning to leave. On his way from the chamber, he grabbed Joseph by the arm. 'Get the boy *out!*'

Joseph nodded and, after watching Kila walk from the chamber, gathered the remaining 10 knights and led the way towards James.

'We must protect you,' said Joseph, staring blankly into James's eyes.

'Protect me?'

Joseph held out a hand. 'Come with me if you want to live.'

★

Outside, Kila paced towards Gilbert, who looked annoyed. 'You're a minute late,' he said.

Kila looked at Queen Belle, then at Gilbert. 'Let her go,' he demanded.

'I think not,' replied Gilbert sharply. 'You are in no position to negotiate.'

Kila stared at Gilbert, uncertain how to proceed. 'Then how will this work?' he shouted, waving his arms in the air.

'A straight swap,' said Gilbert, inching forward, his eyes alight. 'You throw the diamond on the ground and I'll release your queen.'

Kila produced the diamond from the back of his belt.

Gilbert's eyes shone like stars. He knew that the final diamond of Orchestra, the last piece of the jigsaw, was now tantalisingly close. 'Throw it on the ground,' he ordered, his eyes glancing back and forth between Kila and the diamond.

Kila slid the diamond far beyond everyone.

Gilbert looked suspicious. 'Nothing stupid, Kila,' he warned.

Kila was raging. 'I've kept my half of the bargain. Now *let her go!*'

Gilbert nodded at the Volen, who unbound Queen Belle and flung her roughly to the ground.

Kila helped the queen to her feet. 'Are you alright, Your Majesty?'

The Volen ran and picked up the diamond before giving it to Gilbert, who held the sparkling jewel up high and examined it carefully, bringing it closer to his eyes in an effort to detect even the slightest difference that would indicate the diamond to be a fake.

Suddenly he smiled – it was definitely the diamond, identical to the other two. 'Nice to see you again, Kila,' he said, smiling with contentment as he slipped the diamond into his coat pocket. Then he turned and walked away.

Kila needed to know one more thing and called out, 'If Queen Abigail is such a powerful force, why hasn't she shown herself all these years?'

Gilbert turned around, looking very pleased with himself. 'Oh, she will,' he said. 'She most certainly will now.'

Then he disappeared into the Zaran forest.

Guiding Queen Belle across the courtyard, Kila made his way into the palace, closing and bolting the door behind him when he entered. Then, fully expecting a war, he got prepared.

★

Gilbert arrived at the gigantic boats, green light flashing across the ocean as he clutched the diamond victoriously in his hand.

At the mere sight of the powerful jewel, the Volens dropped to their knees in worship.

Gilbert smiled, watching the entire army of Volens bowing their heads, afraid to even look at the diamond. He felt empowered.

After a moment, he placed the diamond into his pocket and tapped the fabric of his coat a couple of times as if to check the diamond was safely inside. 'I have it,' he said loudly.

Seeing that the lights had died, the Volens' rose to their feet and looked at Gilbert, who sensed an appetite for war in each of their eyes.

He brought his hand to his eyebrows, blocking out the sun, and, peering out into the Orchestra Ocean, saw boats full of Volens, all of them wielding swords. Then, he raised his eyes to the heavens and noted that the sky was filled with fearsome Dakotas. 'Kill them all!' he ordered.

This was exactly what the Volens had been waiting to hear. Without delay, they jumped from their boats and, knives in mouths, ran towards the palace. At the same time, the Dakotas soared through the air, the motion of their huge wings generating waves on the ocean.

When all was quiet again, Gilbert stood still, watching the waves rocking to and fro, until they stopped completely and the surface of the ocean fell flat again.

All was calm now.

Breathing heavily, scarcely able to believe the moment had arrived, he lifted out the diamond and looked at it. It had been 11 long years since he had last held a diamond of Orchestra and even then he had been parted from it all too quickly.

Now, he was going to enjoy every moment. He cupped the diamond in his two hands and brought it closer to his face, not daring to blink. He stroked the facets with his fingertips. *Beautiful! The diamond is mine, nobody else's. All mine.* Then, holding the sparkling diamond in the air, he laughed uproariously.

★

The 11 knights, along with Grampian, had rushed James to the back of the palace, where they had opened a window in preparation for his escape.

Joseph looked at James, pointed to the sky and said, 'You must leave.'

'They will surely attack the palace,' said Noah.

Just then, as predicted, humming erupted around the palace and the knights looked at each other despairingly.

'You must all fly to safety,' said Tobias, glancing over his shoulder.

James sighed. 'I can't just leave!'

'James,' said Lance, 'your welfare is far more important than the diamond or anything else at this moment in time.'

'He's right, James,' said Joel. 'You're much too young. It is not your time to fight.'

'Besides,' added Eric, taking out his sword, 'have you seen us fight? We can look after ourselves.' He pointed out the window. 'Now, please, just go.'

'They're right, James,' said Ben.

Reluctantly, James grabbed hold of Ben and Mary's wrists and flew to safety, his eyes lingering back at the 11 knights, who were still watching him closely.

Suddenly, the humming of the Volens grew louder and the knights could hear the gates of the palace being smashed with a battering ram.

Bravely, they unsheathed their swords and ran towards danger.

CHAPTER FIFTY-FIVE

Battle Begins

James glided gracefully through the air but, over time, his flight had become noticeably slower. Hovering in mid-air, he looked deeply concerned.

Ben picked up on it. 'What is it?'

James looked back at the palace, barely visible now in the distance. His conscience had been troubling him for some time. *What kind of a saviour runs?*

'Don't tell me you're thinking of going back,' said Ben.

'No, he's not.' Mary shook her head. 'Isn't that right, James?'

James said nothing; he just kept his eyes fixed on the palace. If he was this supreme warrior and saviour to the people, why were the knights so insistent that he leave? Did they think he wasn't ready? Or perhaps it was more alarming than that. Had they made a mistake – got the wrong person?

Whatever the reason, he was sick and tired of hiding and running. After all, only this morning the knights had praised him – if he remembered correctly, they had told him to start believing in himself and congratulated him on defeating Kila.

And yet, only minutes ago, they had sent him away, banished him, told him he wasn't ready. This didn't make any sense. The very reason he had been scrambled out of Orchestra as a baby was to one day return and help Zara in times like this.

But now here he was, fleeing in the other direction. Well, it just wouldn't do! Lowering into a lush field, he looked at Ben. 'I can't do it! I can't just leave them. I have to go back.'

Ben didn't like what he was hearing. 'What the hell is wrong with you?'

Admittedly, James knew he was in a dilemma. It was a double-edged sword. Keep flying and he was a coward; go back and he would be branded a fool.

Mary said, somewhat sheepishly, 'The knights wanted us to be safe.'

'Blondie's right,' said Ben. 'Going back is out of the question.'

An inspired idea suddenly came to James. He smiled, wondering how he hadn't thought of this earlier. This was a much better plan.

Ben frowned. 'What?'

'Queen Abigail must be all alone in Darken,' James muttered to himself.

Ben looked far from impressed.

James ignored him and turned to Mary. 'Don't you know what this means?' He leaned closer to her, his eyes widening. 'I could get the diamonds back and free the prisoners.' He could see the shock on Mary's face even before he had finished speaking. 'I have to do something!'

'Not something stupid like that,' cried Ben. 'I mean, there's no chance that she's all alone in Darken.'

'What would you have me do then?' James was furious now. 'Run? Hide?'

'Yes,' said Ben, nodding.

James shook his head sadly.

'You're always right, James, aren't you?' said Ben.

'What are you going on about?'

'You're following your ego here, not your head,' said Ben. 'Don't you see? Freeing the prisoners, finding the diamonds – it's all nonsense. It's a trap. They're luring you in. Let it go, James. Let it go!'

James, about to fly, was suddenly halted by Ben's outstretched hand.

'I'm begging you, James, *please* don't do it.'

James looked Ben stubbornly in the eye. 'I've gotten us this far. We'll do this my way!' Then, grabbing hold of Ben's wrist, he flew towards Darken.

★

Inside the palace, the 12 knights stood behind the main door, looking resolute and feeling ready for whatever appeared.

Kila was poised, his sword clasped tightly in his right hand, a look of determination etched on his face. Knowing the time to fight was at hand, he turned to his fellow knights. 'COURAGE! HAVE NO FEAR AND WE WILL WIN THIS WAR!'

At that moment, a battering ram shattered the palace doors and Volens came streaming through, some on all fours, while others ran upright with swords and daggers grasped fiercely in their hands.

Pointing their swords out in from of them, the knights, led by Kila, charged towards the animals, killing many in quick succession.

Running out into the courtyard, Kila was met by a flying fist which connected with his cheekbone. His head rocked to the side and the wind whistled through his teeth. He fell to the ground, rolled, then got back to his feet, his eyes wild with rage.

Adrenalin arrived, generating a quick response. He threw himself at the Volen, severing a leg with the first swipe of his sword and a lower arm with the second.

At the same time, the hum of a running Volen mixed with the screams of the dying one, and Kila, acting on instinct, turned.

Lifting a dagger from his belt, he flung it at the Volen, then watched as the weapon shot through the air and lodged into the animal's shoulder.

Writhing around the ground in agony, the Volen managed to pull the weapon cleanly from the wound before charging back at Kila with the bloody dagger.

Kila, as ruthless as ever, returned, thrusting the point of his sword like a knife through butter into the Volen's body.

As he was removing the blade, he felt two large hands grab him from behind.

From the depths of his heart came hatred, spiteful and vengeful; the type that made him feel so powerful.

He welcomed it.

Gasping for breath, he tossed the Volen over his back, lifted his sword and cut the Volen open with the precision of a surgeon using a scalpel.

Retracting his sword, he looked almost amused; the smile of a man who enjoyed the thrill of battle. Then he finished the screaming animal off, feeling blood splatter across his face, which half blinded him.

At the far side of the courtyard, Joseph fired arrow after arrow, picking Dakotas off with ease.

One Dakota, however, still remained a problem.

High up, and well out of Joseph's range, the elusive creature threw a spear that tore through Noah's thigh and came out the back of his leg, sending him to the ground in excruciating pain.

Kila shouldered a Volen out of his way and rushed over to his friend, who immediately stretched a bloody finger towards the sky.

Raising his eyes, Kila saw the source of the problem. Without a moment's hesitation, he made his move.

Dodging daggers and spears with his reflexes, he raced towards the palace. He feigned right and darted left, missing arrows by inches. Getting closer to the palace entrance, he sensed his task had become much more difficult – a Volen was brandishing a sword and running towards him.

The Volen was not on all fours, but running upright like a man.

Head down, wasting no time, Kila ran straight for the beast, his hands weaponless.

As they drew nearer, the Volen swung his sword at Kila, who arched his upper body backwards, feeling the point of the sword graze the flesh of his chest.

Kila now knew he had the upper hand as the Volen had committed himself. In one brutal move, he whipped his fist through the air and struck the Volen with a crushing blow.

Primed, he waited for the animal to get up, but the Volen remained motionless.

Turning his attention back to the sky, he ran unchallenged into the palace, climbed several flights of stairs and dashed towards the door of the balcony. Entering, his determined eyes found the Dakota hovering in the air.

It was quite a jump to get to the creature. Kila, however, fancied his chances.

Showing tremendous courage, he hurled himself from the balcony and landed on the back of the Dakota, grasping its neck tightly to avoid falling. The creature shook its head violently, trying to shake Kila off.

With his legs dangling dangerously in mid-air, Kila hoisted a knife from his belt and plunged the weapon into the creature's neck.

At once, the lifeless creature plummeted towards the harsh courtyard far below.

Aware that the Dakota would break his fall, Kila just clung on tightly and waited for the collision.

A moment later, the large creature hit the ground with crushing force, sending dust into the air. Staggering to his feet, Kila fought for his breath but took little time to recover as he lifted a sword from the ground and rushed towards an oncoming Volen with the weapon outstretched.

★

When the children had arrived at the outskirts of Darken, Ben and Mary stood looking at the two forests either side of the lane, while James had already taken a few steps forward, his eyes alight with anticipation. *My destiny.*

Mary was beside herself with worry. 'We shouldn't be here, James,' she said, glancing nervously around.

'She's right,' said Ben. 'This is madness, James. What were you thinking? Kila told us to get to safety. What would he think if he saw us here? Let's just leave.'

Turning to Ben and Mary, James said, 'I won't ask you to come any further. I'm going to the castle and I'm not leaving until I've freed every single prisoner. If I come across the diamonds then great, that will be a bonus.'

Ben couldn't believe what he had just heard. 'Are you crazy? You heard what Nathan said – you're not ready yet.'

'I have to,' replied James.

'Is this about that stupid prophecy?' shouted Ben.

James glanced sheepishly at Ben, barely able to look him in the eye.

'Listen, James,' Ben went on, 'prophecies are like rules – they're made to be broken.'

James shook his head.

'You're not ready yet,' Ben pleaded.

James rounded on them. 'Look, if these people believe in me so much, maybe I should start believing in myself. I have to do this.'

Ben looked into James's determined eyes and sighed.

James looked at them. 'Here,' he said, holding out his hands, his tone softening, 'I'll fly you back down the mountain.'

Moments later, James flew deep into the Zaran forest, but made sure everywhere was safe before placing Ben and Mary on the leafy ground.

'Please be careful, James,' said Mary.

Ben grimaced. 'She probably has an army bigger than the one at the palace waiting for you.'

James forced a smile. 'Listen, I can fly, remember? If there's any sign of trouble, I'll fly away immediately.'

'Promise?' said Mary timidly, feeling slightly better.

'Promise,' replied James with a smile. Then, with one hand pointed over his head, he rose upwards in zigzags, higher and higher, until finally, feeling delighted with his technique, he stopped and looked down at Ben and Mary, who were waving up at him. He climbed higher and tore through the sky, making steady progress towards Darken.

Minutes later, full of hope and anticipation, the cold wind of Darken not bothering him, James Clyde moved past each tree. His eyes were fixed upon the castle that was now in his sight. Through the light mist, he could see the gates lying open. It almost looked too easy.

A voice from deep within told him it was a trap. Quickly, he looked everywhere. *Deserted!* He smiled, grateful for the instinct that had made him go through with this. His gamble had paid off; he could see that now.

Taking a deep breath, he continued on his way, shifting his thin body between each tree.

Then, getting down on his hunkers, he hid behind the tree nearest the castle and thought about his next move.

★

Kila could barely see. The blood dripping down his brow was not his own, but his vision was still impeded.

Using the sleeve of his shirt, he wiped his face. His vision cleared and he looked around, seeing hundreds of dead Volens and Dakotas lying prostrate around the courtyard. He sighed, savouring the victory.

Smiling, the knights looked at one another. Then, gathering closer, they roared with triumph.

Kila knew the battle was over, but the war had just begun. Even so, he rejoiced in the moment with his friends.

'We got James to safety, Kila,' said Gabriel, trying to catch his breath.

Bathed in blood, Kila managed to speak. 'You did the right thing,' he said, patting Gabriel strongly on the shoulder.

A moment later, Kila's shattered body fell to the ground, his every muscle now aching. On his knees, he suddenly heard voices calling his name.

Looking towards the Zaran forest, he saw Ben and Mary racing towards him. Sensing something was terribly wrong, Kila jumped to his feet and walked quickly towards them.

The knights were drenched in blood and the courtyard was hardly a sight for a child. Concerned about this, Tobias stepped quickly forward and covered Mary's eyes before lifting her into the palace.

'What is it, Ben?' said Kila, moving forward, leaving dead bodies behind him. 'What are you doing here?'

'It's James,' said Ben breathlessly.

'What about James?' Kila looked madly around. 'Where is he?'

'He's gone to Darken to free the prisoners.'

Kila could feel the colour draining from his face. 'He's done *what*?'

CHAPTER FIFTY-SIX

Revenge

Deep inside Darken forest, James, whose eyes had been focused on the castle for some time, now felt confident that the kingdom was free of danger.

All of a sudden, his eyes were drawn towards the forest on his right and the rustling of leaves. Though he could see very little, he knew Gilbert too well not to recognise him.

Emerging from the misty forest, the man in black strode forward confidently, the last diamond of Orchestra held aloft in his hand.

A smile formed on James's face. It was time to finish this once and for all.

He thought about his grandfather. He thought about the father he had never known.

Above all else, he thought about killing the man in black.

CHAPTER FIFTY-SEVEN

The Legendary James Clyde

Gilbert's lips curled into a smile. 'The legendary James Clyde, I presume.'

James gave a nod, and Gilbert added, 'We meet at last.'

'I want the diamonds!' James brandished his sword and pointed the tip towards the diamond clutched in Gilbert's hand. 'I'll start with that one.'

There was a moment of tense silence. 'Boy, you are making a terrible mistake,' said Gilbert, finally. 'You've allowed yourself to be tricked and brainwashed.'

'Really?'

Gilbert heaved a sigh. 'The knights have deluded you with lies, James. I know only too well how you feel. They believe in you so strongly, and yet this is based on nothing more than rumours and myths.'

Remaining silent, James stared at Gilbert in anger.

Gilbert held the diamond outward. 'The war is over; we have won. Once the ritual is complete, I will have power over the land.'

Sword held tightly before him, James moved a fraction closer to Gilbert. 'You will have nothing,' he said. 'Your queen isn't interested in you; she's only interested in power.'

Gilbert looked down at the diamond. 'And you're not?' He put the diamond in his pocket. 'This is your last chance. Turn around, go back to where you came from and pretend that a place called Orchestra never existed. If you do that, you will live.'

James stood his ground, but for the very first time since entering Darken, he felt fear.

'Boy, I am offering you your life,' said Gilbert. 'Take it. Go home.'

James's grip tightened around the hilt of his sword. 'I am home.'

Gilbert had had enough. 'So be it,' he said. 'But let it be known, I did try to reason with you.'

James suddenly realised that the man in black's coat was unbuttoned and flapping in the breeze.

Something wasn't right.

Gilbert took two quick steps forward. 'So, the knights believe you're the promised saviour. Well then, let's find out!'

Out of nowhere, a thunderous bang reverberated across Orchestra, sending frightened crows squawking from the trees.

James jumped. As he wondered what the sound might've been, he felt a sudden chill, which was soon accompanied by a searing pain.

His hand began to tremble and he just had to let go of his sword. Looking down, he saw droplets of blood fall on to the steel. *My blood!*

Instinctively, his hand fled to his stomach. He could feel warm blood seeping through his fingers. His legs went from under him and he dropped to his knees.

Then, head bowed, he collapsed completely.

Satisfied that the task was complete, Gilbert put the smoky pistol callously into his pocket. Then, buttoning his coat, he walked towards the castle gates as if nothing had ever happened. 'Foolish boy,' he muttered, walking inside.

★

The knights of Zara were on horseback, galloping at a relentless speed through the Zaran forest.

Kila and the children led the way. Mary sat in the middle, just in front of Ben, with Kila taking the reins.

Moments ago, they had all heard a loud bang and had looked at one another nervously.

'What was that?' Kila had asked, slowing up his frightened horse.

'It sounded like a gunshot,' said Ben tensely.

Kila looked worried. 'What's a gunshot?'

'Believe me,' said Mary, 'you don't want to know.'

The knights' powerful white horses darted in between the trees. When they had reached the end of Orchestra Ocean, the knights pulled the reins back and stopped, their horses neighing.

'Not far now,' said Ben.

'Which way?' shouted Kila.

Ben gestured to a steep bank. 'That way!'

At once, Kila cracked the reins of his horse and the marvellous animal climbed the embankment with ease.

As he looked up, Kila felt a sudden rise of sadness. Although it had been many years since he had last set foot in Darken, the place he remembered was warm and joyful. What he now found himself staring at held none of those qualities.

Something told him that James Clyde wasn't ready to be in a place like this. He raised himself up in his stirrups and peered around, looking for James, but he couldn't see him.

'I hate Darken,' muttered Ben, the wind ruffling his hair.

Letting out a roar, Kila snapped the reins of his horse and quickened the pace.

The rest of the knights followed closely behind as they all raced through the forest, hoping that they would make it to James before it was too late.

CHAPTER FIFTY-EIGHT

Nobody Is Coming For You

Lying on his back with his hands placed on his stomach, James knew it was the same position his grandfather had died in.

But the similarities didn't end there: it was the same wound, the same killer and the same horrible slow death. The irony was upsetting. Who would avenge his grandfather now?

As he lay there pondering this question, he thought he could hear the sound of footsteps on the gravel. For a brief moment, he felt hope. '*Help me,*' he groaned, but soon he saw the large form of a Volen standing over him.

'Look! The saviour of Orchestra is begging for help.'

A group of Volens came forward and looked down at James with interest. 'Is this the child whose birth was foretold?' one of them asked.

'No, it can't be,' argued another. 'Look, he's bleeding. This boy is mortal.'

A Volen broke through the crowd, a black patch covering his right eye. 'This *is* James Clyde,' he shouted. 'Everyone take a good look.'

One by one they came forward.

'This proves one thing,' the Volen went on. 'The prophecies of Orchestra were nothing more than a hoax; a story created to give the people of Orchestra hope.'

The Volens erupted into a mixture of laughter and cheers.

When the noise had finally subsided, the Volen with only one good eye dropped to his knees and, using the handle of his sword, clubbed James across the head, slicing open a wound. 'That's for giving people false hope,' he said angrily. 'You were given a chance to walk. You should've taken it!'

A droplet of blood ran down James's brow and the Volen caught it with a knife. 'So the great saviour bleeds after all. Listen, powerful saviour. Do you hear that sound?'

James could hear nothing.

'That is the sound of silence,' the Volen said in a coaxing tone of voice. 'You do realise that nobody is coming for you? No divine intervention.' Hands raised, he turned to the crowd of onlookers. 'It would appear the saviour isn't worth saving after all.'

The Volen looked down at James's bloodied body. 'Goodbye, James Clyde – King of Orchestra.' He tightened his grip on the sword in his hand and prepared to deliver the fatal blow.

James Clyde lay on the ground motionless; he watched as the sword descended and clenched his eyes closed, resigned to his fate.

- CHAPTER FIFTY-NINE -

Mary's Gift

Although he had resigned himself to death, James Clyde had *nothing* to fear. For out of the forest, through the thickening mist, came Kila.

The Volen driving the sword downwards could never have seen the dagger that plunged into the back of his skull, but his last thought was of Kila.

Somehow, without even seeing who had thrown the blade, he knew that his life had been taken by the great knight.

'It's Kila!' a Volen called out.

James's heart lifted when he heard the name.

As Kila dismounted his horse, the surrounding mist gave him a supernatural look, adding to his already fearsome image.

Fuelled by rage, he ran forward, slashing his sword at terrified Volens and Dakotas, killing them instantly. He punched another Volen, feeling his bruised and bloody knuckles shattering the animal's jaw.

Another Volen rushed towards him.

SLASH!

The animal's leg was *gone*, sliced below the knee. The Volen was screaming and feeling for a leg that was no longer there; instead, his hand found a gushing stump.

With defeat looming, the remaining Darken army dispersed.

Kila knelt down beside James. It looked pretty bad. Blood was everywhere, as if James had been dipped into red paint. 'Don't speak, James. Just hold on, I'm going to get you out of here.' Quickly, he removed his outer garment and, with the help of Joseph, wrapped it round James's waist; he then tied a knot and made sure no blood was seeping through.

With that done, he laid James carefully across his horse, jumped on to the saddle of his noble steed and led the rest of the knights back the way they had travelled.

Entering the palace minutes later, Kila carried James effortlessly in his arms, all the while praying for a miracle.

As he headed for the glass table in the middle of the dining chamber, he shouted, 'Grampian, where are you? I need help.' He lowered James gently on to the table and took a step back, watery-eyed and drained.

All 11 knights circled the table in despair and watched as Kila untied his garment from around James's waist, exposing the scorched skin.

When they saw the bullet wound, some knights cringed, while others gasped or turned away. They had never seen anything like it before. To their shock, the wound was still spurting blood.

Although Kila hoped he was wrong, years of experience told him that James Clyde had only moments to live. Wanting to be with him at the end, Kila lifted his fingers from the wound, allowing the blood to flow freely. With tearful eyes, he held James softly by the hand.

At the same time, James tried to say something, but his voice was getting feeble and his once sky-blue eyes had become dull and lifeless.

Feeling his pain subside, he could've sworn he heard the deep voice of his grandfather speaking softly in his ear, reassuring him that all would be well.

As the whisper slowly faded, he turned and looked up at the magnificent fresco decorated into the domed-shaped ceiling of the palace.

Strangely, he had never noticed this decoration on the ceiling before, but he felt drawn to it now.

It was simply beautiful.

The fresco was painted to resemble the sky, with pigments of blue and white used flawlessly to give the visual impression that there was no ceiling at all.

Suddenly a blinding light flashed from the painted sky. Glancing at Kila and the knights standing over him, James suddenly realised that only he could see this light.

The glow became more intense, then vanished and a white figure emerged, smiling.

'Hello, James. Do you remember me?'

'How could I forget?' replied James, who now found himself standing beside the glowing spirit. 'I knew you were an angel.' He ran his fingertips along the beautifully textured ceiling. Then looking down, he hung his head. 'I've let you down.'

The mighty being before him spoke like a kind, caring mother forgiving her beloved son. 'No, you haven't,' she said. 'You will still be a great king and rule Orchestra with kindness and compassion. But you must go back and finish what has started. It is not your time, James, and you must go back.'

James shook his head sadly, as he wanted to stay with her forever, but then he remembered Ben and Mary.

'He's gone,' said Noah in a trembling voice, his sad eyes fixed on Kila, who looked distraught as he held James's lifeless body in his thick arms.

Noah was right – James Clyde was dead. The unthinkable had happened.

Ben, crying heavily, felt his arm being pulled. When he saw it was Mary, he moved out of her way.

Kila laid James back on the table and watched as Mary placed one hand on James's brow and the other on the bullet wound, which incredibly showed instant signs of healing.

A moment later, she smiled, feeling satisfied with her work.

Lifting her hand away, she peered down. The blood had stopped flowing and the bullet wound had vanished miraculously.

Slowly, James opened his eyes, feeling refreshed. He gazed up at Mary, who was holding his head kindly. He peered around and saw familiar faces – Ben was leaning over the table while the knights of Zara and the orchins of Orchestra stood a little further back, keeping a keen eye on him. He turned his eyes towards the ceiling, but the spirit was gone.

Mary gave him a hug. 'Guess what gift I chose?'

James nodded, studying her hands. 'I don't know how to thank you.'

'You're here now,' Mary replied warmly. 'That's all I could ever want.'

Ben edged closer to the table and hesitated, looking down at James, wanting to make sure he was back to full health. 'Are you alright?' he said, wiping his eyes with his sleeve.

James nodded. 'I'm fine.'

Then, gathering together, all three children held each other tightly.

A while later, the knights of Zara approached.

'Welcome back,' said Kila with a smile, as he and the other knights peered down at James. 'I have someone you might like to meet.'

James could hear footsteps. When he raised his head, he saw a blonde-haired lady with blue eyes, much like his own, walking quickly towards him. Her smile was radiant and James smiled broadly back. 'You're my mum, aren't you?'

Before James got an answer, the woman had gripped him in a tight embrace. He could feel her tears on his cheeks.

Then he realised that he too was crying.

CHAPTER SIXTY

It Has Been Accomplished

Gilbert marched triumphantly up the great hall of Darken Castle, a proud look upon his face.

'Report,' Queen Abigail said sharply.

Gilbert knelt, then rose, smiling broadly. 'It has been accomplished.'

Queen Abigail's eyes widened. 'You have the diamond?'

Gilbert nodded, pulled the magnificent diamond from his coat pocket and said, 'I do, Your Majesty.'

Imorex sat up, his eyes riveted on the diamond.

'Bring it to me!' Queen Abigail ordered, refusing to believe her eyes until the elusive diamond was in her hands.

Gilbert made his way up the central aisle and passed her the diamond.

Standing up, Queen Abigail noticed that more light was required for an accurate examination.

She pointed her right index finger at numerous sets of candle stands that were positioned all around the stone walls of the castle. Each one burst into flames at her silent command.

Hurrying, she went to the back of her throne, got down on her knees, and slid open a secret compartment. Reaching inside, she lifted out two more diamonds and moved them around like a child playing with marbles.

'It's over!'

Without doubt, the diamonds were identical – right down to the exact crevice. A look of sheer joy appeared on her face. 'I will rule on high.'

The great hall flickered with lights of emerald green as the queen returned to her throne. Her excited eyes found Gilbert. 'And what of the boy?'

'Dead, Your Majesty,' replied Gilbert. 'I took care of him myself.'

Imorex glanced at Gilbert suspiciously.

Queen Abigail's smile returned. This was the assurance she sought. 'Your reward will be great, Gilbert. Your voice will be second only to my own in this land. You have served me well and loyally. I promised you power all those years ago and now you shall have it.'

Gilbert nodded and smiled.

The queen looked down again, studying the once mythological diamonds of Orchestra nestled in her palms. She had tasted the power of the diamonds twice now.

The third, she knew, would be the sweetest one of them all, but more than that, the three diamonds could now be combined. The ultimate reward. *Immortality.* Everlasting life would soon be claimed.

And yet, one final hurdle still had to be overcome: the ritual itself. The sooner it was over, the better. Smiling, she tightened her grip on the diamonds and stood up from her throne.

★

In Zara, James had now fully recovered and was resting in his bed with Ben and Mary by his side.

James smiled at them. 'We've come a long way, haven't we?'

'We've had quite an adventure, Jimbo,' said Ben.

Gabriel knocked on the door but didn't wait for a response and breezed into the chamber, wearing a broad smile. 'Look at that,' he said, nodding at James. 'Feeling better?'

James smiled. 'Much, thanks.'

'Good. Hungry?'

'Erm, not really.'

'Good, because Kila wants to speak to you.'

'Okay,' said James. 'Is he downstairs?'

Gabriel frowned. 'No, it requires a little flying, I'm afraid. He's waiting for you at the top of the mountain.'

James felt this strange. 'Why the mountain?'

Gabriel shrugged. 'I don't know,' he replied. 'Are you feeling up to it?'

James glided from his bed and drifted towards the balcony doors.

Gabriel took this as a yes and left the chamber.

James was now moving as if he had never been shot. He stopped to look back at Ben and Mary. 'Will you both be here when I come back?'

Mary smiled. 'Yep, we can't fly away – unlike some.'

James walked out on to the balcony and was about to fly into the air when he suddenly remembered something he had been meaning to ask Ben. 'Ben, if Mary has the gift of healing, what did you wish for?'

Ben was smiling. 'No chance I'm telling you. I think I'll keep that a secret for a little longer. Besides, you never know when it might come in handy.'

Mary went over to where James stood. She held his hand softly and they both gazed out across Orchestra.

The Zaran forest stood below in all its grandeur. A beautiful rainbow had developed over the trees, causing Mary to remember their great friend. 'Rainbow,' she muttered to herself. 'Simon Rainbow.' She spoke louder this time, just to make sure that James and Ben heard her.

James felt guilty; his former life seemed like a vague dream at this stage.

'He must be really worried about us,' said Ben, walking over to the balcony.

Mary nodded.

James Clyde smiled, as he often did when he thought of Simon Rainbow.

'We have to get him,' suggested Mary.

'He would love it here, James,' added Ben.

James looked at them. 'We'll return and bring our good friend back with us to Orchestra.'

'For good?' said Mary.

James laughed. 'Well, for a short holiday to begin with.' He nudged Ben in the ribs. 'Go find Grampian and tell him we'll need a transporter at once.'

'What's a transporter?' asked Mary with interest.

James smiled. 'Oh, you just wait and see,' he told her.

As Ben and Mary ran out the chamber door, they had a wonderful feeling that they were about to embark on another adventure.

James stood on the railing of the balcony, a faint current of cool air brushing his face. He noticed the change in temperature immediately; there was actually a nip in the air.

Moreover, the whole landscape appeared to have changed from green to bronze. He wondered if the seasons had changed. Did Orchestra have seasons? He had no idea. There was still so much more he had to find out about this amazing land.

His hands on his hips, he took off, gliding from the balcony with the grace of a bird escaping from a cage.

As he soared through the clouds, he started to wonder what Kila could possibly want with him.

When he flew nearer to the mountain, the realisation of the situation suddenly dawned on him.

Darken had acquired all three diamonds of Orchestra. Whatever bargaining power Zara once had with one diamond was now gone.

Any day now, Darken would be back to finish the job. This thought made him feel very disheartened. As he rose to the top of the mountain, he fully expected Kila to be fuming with him.

Gliding upwards, he could see Kila standing majestically at the mountain's edge, overlooking the breathtaking land of Orchestra, like a protective father keeping an eye on his children.

'You wanted to see me, Kila?' said James, calmly as possible.

Kila nodded. 'Yes, James.' He pointed forward. 'Take a look out there.'

James turned, peered downwards and let himself absorb the scenery of his kingdom. The sun had slackened; the strength of its rays were more like autumn than summer and, without the blinding glare, he could see everywhere.

He saw Orchestra Ocean stretch out for miles and heard the roar of the powerful waterfall below his feet. It was a sight of grandeur he knew his eyes would never truly get used to. 'Outstanding,' he said, finally.

'That it is, James,' said Kila, looking out. 'And it's all yours.'

James reddened and said, 'I know you're disappointed in me. I've let you down. I failed.'

Kila was shaking his head. 'James, we are winning.'

James looked up. 'But Kila, they have the three diamonds of Orchestra.'

Kila smiled. 'They think you're dead, but you are alive,' he said. 'You still have much to learn and you will. You're young. One day, you'll claim your revenge. That I promise you.' He laid a comforting hand on James's shoulder.

Feeling better already, James looked up at the iconic Kila, hoping one day to be just like him. 'You're like a father to me, Kila,' he said. 'You know that, I hope?'

Kila gave a nod. 'Go. Go back to Ben and Mary. Have fun and play games. I might even give you the day off from training.'

James held a hand outward. 'I'll give you a lift down.'

'No chance,' said Kila with a loud laugh. 'I'll walk, thank you very much.'

'I'll see you later, then?' said James, his eyes beaming.

Kila smiled. 'Of course.'

James walked over to the edge and prepared for take-off, only to be disturbed suddenly when he heard the faint cry of an orchin running frantically through the flowers, her hands waving furiously in the air.

The little orchin arrived out of breath and covered in petals, but she still managed to get her point across. 'This is for you,' she said breathlessly, handing James a brown paper-covered parcel fastened by a string of red rope.

James looked at the orchin curiously as he noticed the present was some sort of cloth, a jumper perhaps.

'It's a present from Grampian,' said the orchin, still panting.

With great interest, James ripped the parcel open and stared down at the strawberry-red cloth before him. 'What is it?' he said, looking down at the orchin.

'It's a cape,' the orchin told him, looking very proud. 'We all made it.'

James let the cape unravel and it flowed majestically to the ground. The cape attached below his shoulders and ran all the way down to the soles of his white boots.

'An outfit made for a king,' said Kila.

James patted the orchin kindly on the head and walked over to the edge of the mountain.

'James,' Kila called out.

James turned, and Kila said, 'You won't venture too far, will you?'

James's eyes narrowed. 'Why?'

'We don't want to lose you again. Please just say you'll be around.'

James nodded, smiling. 'I'll always be around.'

And so, for *perhaps* the very last time, James ran and jumped from the mountaintop, the spray of the ceaseless waterfall hitting his face.

Like a cork leaving a bottle, he shot downwards, his head bowed, his arms by his side. Breaking through the surface of the water, he dove to the very bottom of the ocean.

Then, with one hand pointed above his head, he powered straight back up through the water and into the air, his newly acquired red cape flapping heroically behind him.

The birds were flying along with him and the dolphins were following far below, almost mirroring his every move. He produced his sword, swished it through the air and let out a roar as he soared higher towards the golden clouds.

He was free. He knew he would have many more adventures with the evil Gilbert and the scheming Queen Abigail, but for now he was happy to be home.

Yes, James Clyde was here to stay.

CHAPTER SIXTY-ONE

Not Over Yet

At Darken Castle, Queen Abigail had abandoned her throne to start the ritual with the diamonds of Orchestra.

Gilbert still remained in the great hall.

The sorcerer Imorex was there. Gilbert's face wore a smile and he seemed to be basking in the moment. *It's finally over,* he told himself. *We have won.*

Imorex looked sadly at him. 'Are you sure you killed the boy, Gilbert?'

'I am,' replied Gilbert with a confident nod. 'I saw it with my own two eyes. He wasn't the person they thought he was after all.' He suddenly sensed sadness in the sorcerer's demeanour. 'Why do you ask me old one?'

Imorex looked straight into Gilbert's eyes and said, 'We might have a problem.'

Epilogue

For the last two days, Wilmore Clyde's house had been under siege by police, reporters and anxious neighbours who feared that a murderer now lived among them.

The mansion was barricaded off, pending further investigation into the murder of Wilmore Clyde and the possible kidnapping of three children.

To make matters worse, there had been no arrests, and the prime suspect in the case couldn't be pinpointed.

The children had just vanished off the face of the earth. Quite frankly, the police were baffled.

Even more puzzling was a motive for such an attack. Although the luxurious house held many enticing artefacts for potential burglars, there was no sign of anything missing.

The assailant, however, had made no effort to disguise his entry; the front door was pulverised, pointing to more than one person involved.

Soon after the events, the detective in charge of the case, a bearded, imposing and well-spoken man called John Brady, went on television and promised that those responsible would be brought to justice.

Forensics had taken fingerprints away for analysis and most samples were concentrated to a room where the only item of note was a large but empty chest.

Also taken for analysis was a letter found in the victim's office. It was a crumpled letter requesting a meeting, signed by a man called Gilbert, who was now the prime suspect.

The letter mentioned a diamond and the police hadn't ruled out the possibility that Wilmore Clyde had been a smuggler.

The man who called himself Gilbert had met Wilmore on the night of the murder. Police urged the man to come forward with information, but as yet there had been no contact made.

A local man called Gilbert Miller had been hounded by neighbours. They wanted him to come forward and admit his guilt, but even after his house had been set on fire, he refused to confess to the murder.

Disenchanted with the whole investigation, Gilbert Miller packed up and left the neighbourhood, vowing never to return again.

Now, the house lay empty and the whereabouts of the children still remained a mystery. The effect of the murder was far-reaching, with every person within a 50 mile radius scared for their own safety.

As soon as the tragedy struck, the local school was closed indefinitely. Mrs Walsh, the children's teacher, came forward with information about a strange man asking questions about James a couple of days before his disappearance. This man couldn't be found, leaving the police with very little to go on.

After the tragic events, Anne Brown was the first person to be questioned. She gave a tearful account of the last time she had been in the children's company. Her story checked out and she was now receiving counselling to help her overcome her grief.

Even Simon Rainbow had been questioned, but the police were quick to stress that he wasn't a suspect.

Since the awful events, Simon hadn't slept or eaten, thinking relentlessly about his friends. He had to investigate for himself.

That evening, after he had wished his parents goodnight, he put two AA batteries into a flashlight, planted his pillow under the duvet of his bed and climbed out the window of his room.

Despite the heavy snow, he ran all the way to Wilmore's house.

When he arrived, he felt sad to see the black gates shut and the surrounding area barricaded with yellow tape.

Beside the gates were bouquets of flowers commemorating the life of Wilmore Clyde.

Simon looked at a few of the kind notes attached to the flowers, but when he felt his eyes becoming moist, he left.

He ignored the *DO NOT ENTER* sign, squeezed through a gap beside the gate and walked up the driveway, the tall garden lamps responding to his footsteps and illuminating the surrounding grounds.

Just ahead, he could see the once-majestic front door replaced by slabs of wood. He could only imagine the terrible events that had happened here.

From his pocket, he took out his flashlight, flicked it on and ventured round to the back of the house, hoping to find an entrance.

When he came to the back of the house, he noticed that one of the numerous windows was partially open.

This was his chance. He prised the frame open and rolled into the house, landing on the wooden floor with a thud.

Getting to his feet, he shone the flashlight around the house in an effort to find his bearings. He let his gaze follow the strong beam of light as it shone on the stone faces of the 12 knights of Zara.

Then he started to walk.

He should have been terrified wandering around a dark house where a murder had been committed, but he was more sad than frightened. He hadn't been there for his friends when they had needed him the most.

He moved soundlessly towards the staircase, half expecting his friends to greet him at any moment, but they never did.

The last particles of snow on the soles of his trainers finally melted as he climbed the first staircase.

When he had climbed another staircase and turned several corners, he came to a stretch of long corridor where a rocking chair sat against the wall.

He felt drawn to this wing of the house, as if his friends were somehow guiding his movements. He shone the flashlight down the long passageway and discovered a single door.

Quickly, he looked all around, trying to see a light or a stir of movement elsewhere, but he could see nothing; just darkness from every corner of the house.

Nevertheless, he truly believed he was making progress. Stopping just before the door, he took a deep breath.

Slowly, he outstretched a hand to turn the doorknob, but as he did this, he heard a familiar voice from inside call out, 'Simon!'

It was *definitely* Mary.

When Simon barged through the door, his eyes were momentarily blinded by a flash of brilliant white light, but when his vision had recovered, he looked up and saw what resembled a treasure chest sitting in the corner of the room with a familiar child now standing in it.

Simon broke into a wide smile and looked like a boy who had just solved the entire mystery surrounding the disappearance of his friends.

Maybe he just had.